INTO ELURIEN

Kate Sparkes

Sparrowcat Press

Publisher's Note: This is a work of fiction. Names, characters, places, and incidents are a product of the author's imagination. Locales and public names are sometimes used for atmospheric purposes. Any resemblance to actual people, living or dead, or to businesses, companies, events, institutions, or locales is completely coincidental.

Book Layout ©2013 BookDesignTemplates.com

Into Elurien/ Kate Sparkes. -- 1st print ed.
ISBN 978-0-9949999-4-8

For Krista
Thanks for holding my hand, talking me down off of ledges, and understanding all of the hard parts of this job.

1

"It was a dark and stormy night..." Such a cliché, and not the way to begin a proper story. But the fact remains that it was both dark and stormy on the night I returned to my hometown—an ominous beginning, if you believe in that sort of thing.

And I truly did.

The rabbit's foot hanging from my rearview mirror swung in crazy arcs as Gladys, a Volkswagen outdated enough to have earned a proper old dame moniker, bounced over the potholes I couldn't avoid at the end of the causeway. It had been a harsh winter this year. I knew this because my mother's daily demotivational emails kept me on top of all the Fairbrook gossip during my years away. She had, however, neglected to remind me of how the local crews didn't bother to fix anything at this end of the island until it was time to prepare for tourist season. Small town charm was a bankable commodity only from June to November. The rest of the year, the island curled up in curmudgeonly isolation in a sheltered spot off the northern shore of Newfoundland, secure in the knowledge that those seeking the illusion of a simpler lifestyle would return in the summer to spread their dollars and snap their photos.

I took the rabbit's foot down and tossed it on the passenger seat. Not a cheap trinket, that. This was the real deal—left hind foot, shot by a cross-eyed man in a cemetery. The lucky limb (*Not so lucky for the rabbit,* I reflected) landed on the leather cover of my Filofax. They might have seemed like an odd pairing to some. My perfectly organized life, planned to the hour and plotted years ahead, versus the implication that fate and bad luck could screw it all up at any moment. But the thing is, both are about control. Why would I worry about my detailed plans and then run the risk of them being derailed because I walked under a ladder?

Plans. Fail-safes. Lucky charms. It's all superstition, when you think about it. All ways to make us feel better about the future when in reality we have so little control. Lack of control made me jittery. I grabbed onto it where I could.

I squinted through early spring rain that Gladys's windshield wipers couldn't keep up with. Coming at night had been a stupid idea.

But then, I hadn't planned to come back to Fairbrook at all. My sneakers had left tread-marks on the road as I tore out of town after graduation, and by October I'd lost touch with everyone from high school. I had cared for my friends on the island, as they had for me, but the larger world beckoned some of us. I'd planned a successful academic career that would finally make my parents proud, followed by... Well, I'd never really decided that, but I knew it didn't involve Fairbrook. I went to school, I did well, and I even allowed a boyfriend to worm his way into my life on the basis of common interests, a promising future, and crazy attraction.

And then I got sick and took a year off, not in any position to care that doing so would mean I had to start paying off my student loans. I'd hopped from job to meaningless job, struggling to make ends meet, telling my parents that everything was fine so I wouldn't have to hear the sighs and the *why didn't you*s and the *I told you that you would never*s. Those lies fell apart when Jake and I broke up and I lost my home. I'd managed to set myself up in a short-term rental for a few months, but money quickly ran short.

I tried to put a positive spin on things, but I knew my mother had seen through it when she mentioned that Uncle Harry needed someone to manage the dairy bar. The seasonal job with great pay and solid benefits was mine for the taking.

I took it. Where else was I going to go?

The best laid plans, and all that.

Maybe it will be fine, I told myself, ignoring the churning of my stomach as my headlights picked out the big "WELCOME TO FAIRBROOK" sign. *Work here for the summer, take long-distance courses over the winter, get out again when things look brighter.*

I knew it was bullshit. You can't escape a town like Fairbrook without a certain amount of momentum. I had big scholarships when I blew out of there the first time, and even bigger plans. I was dragging my ass back on a quarter tank of gas, a load of debt, and a heart that probably resembled the dented cans on the discount shelf at McMurtry's Grocery.

I could live without Jake. It was my shattered confidence that had me wondering where I'd find the will to leave again.

The road improved as it wound through the old forest. It was skeletal-looking now, but it would have been a breathtaking view back in the autumn, when the last of the sightseers camped or lodged their way through and tagged their works #Fairbrook #fall

#BimbleIsland #AweInspiring and, I assumed, #PayAttentionToMe. I'd heard all about the town meeting regarding which hashtags to encourage and the ensuing confusion over what the hell these "hashbag" things were, anyway.

Fairbrook. A nice place to visit, but God, I did not want to live there.

Gladys picked up speed as I shifted gears. Not too fast, not too high. Jake had never liked the old girl. But then, he'd never bothered to learn to drive standard. I should have taken that as a sign.

The headlights found more signs. The Old Brook Inn, Nana's Nook (*Home-Cooked meals, Seafood our specialty!!*), Barb's B&B. All hand-painted, all homey and quaint, just like Fairbrook was supposed to be, at least when it had its tourist-welcoming makeup on. I paid no attention to the wave of nausea that came at the sight of the Walsh's Dairy sign.

It's going to be great, I promised myself for the hundred-and-twelfth time that day. *You have a plan. You have a promising future ahead of you. You have—*

Gladys hit a bump, and the rabbit foot slid to the floor.

Good luck, I finished sheepishly. I knew it was silly. I didn't care. It made me feel better. *And helping Uncle Harry out should be great karma, or something. And maybe—*

I never got to the maybe. A dark shape moved at the edge of my light. I slammed on the brakes as a mostly grown moose darted into the road and then froze, bright eyes staring at me. Gladys spun sideways, and I fought the urge to wrench the wheel back around. Cold coffee soaked my jeans as the paper cup next to me spilled and my bags tumbled in the back seat.

The car stopped, engine stalling as the moose trotted off into the forest, his path illuminated by my lights.

I cranked the window down, too flustered to think straight. "Thanks, asshole!" I bellowed after the retreating rump. A face full of blowing rain was my only answer. I grumbled to myself as I rolled the window up and pushed my thick hair into place behind my ears.

After some gentle coaxing, Gladys agreed to restart. We made it half a kilometre down the road before the engine light blinked to life.

"No. Not now. Just a little more." My parents lived at the far end of the island, through town and past the farms.

The engine coughed and clunked, but kept running.

"Gladys. Save your hysterics for when we stop. I'm begging you."

Clunk.

"Really? After everything we've been through together?"

She didn't answer.

"Crooked old bitch."

I had to keep going. No one would be along until morning, and maybe not even then. I'd feel silly calling for a taxi at this hour, though I would if I absolutely had to. There was no way I was calling my parents. I eased the car over the bumps without slowing down too much, dodging potholes when I could.

I waited to see the lights outside of Wood's Service Station, but the place was dark when we rounded the corner. *Of course,* I thought. No point keeping things open late at this time of year. If I recalled correctly, Jimmy Wood was running the place now. He'd been in my class. Excessively popular, very big-fish-tiny-pond, with fantastic college prospects. Nice to everyone in public, but kind of a presumptuous dick if he got a girl alone. He'd made sure everyone knew what a prude I was when I rejected him in eleventh grade. Three months later, he'd knocked up Jenny Goss. No one had batted an eye, save for the blue-haired ladies of the local church women's guild. It was just how things went in Fairbrook. Kind of a local tradition. One in every class.

I considered stopping to knock at the door of the two-storey house behind the service station, but all of the lights were out. I gritted my teeth and urged Gladys over the next hill.

The first lights we reached shone bright and warm against the dark, but they weren't exactly a welcoming sight. Old-fashioned lanterns illuminated the wide porch of the Old Brook Inn, a place of local legend. Tourists always heard the pleasant stories about the seasonal workers who had once been housed in the massive structure, the fire that later destroyed the mill, and the way the other townsfolk cared for the workers afterward. They heard about the fairy rings that still appeared every so often on the lawn, and the local story about the little girl who saw the wee fairies dancing on summer nights.

They didn't hear the darker legends. They knew how many lives were lost in the fire, but not the mysterious circumstances surrounding the fire itself. No one talked about the string of suicides that occurred at the inn not long after, or the ghosts that were supposed to haunt the halls.

Or how the little fairy girl went mad before she turned ten, babbling on about monsters and devils, screaming in her sleep.

I shivered and pulled into the roundabout driveway. *Any port in a storm,* I told myself. The outside lights were on, so maybe Mr. or Mrs. James was still awake. If not, I'd be in for a tongue-lashing the likes of which I hadn't experienced since our graduation party, when the innkeepers realized we were all wandering the halls looking for ghosts, scaring the crap out of each other with squeaky floorboards and flickering lights.

Gladys coughed and swooned into silence as she rolled into the empty parking lot, her mental and physical breakdown apparently complete. *Guess that decision's made then.* I fished my rabbit's foot out from under the seat, stuffed my planner into my purse, and located my overnight bag in the back seat.

I was soaked and shivering by the time I reached the door, but seriously considered spending the night on the porch rather than invoking the wrath of Mr. James. The man had devil eyes, my grandmother had once said, and a temper to match.

Maybe I'd count as a tourist now. He'd always been nice to them.

I tried the door and found it locked. The knocker, an old brass thing cast in the shape of a grotesquely squashed fairy face, was heavier than I expected. I rapped three times, and waited.

2

Lights flicked on inside the inn. I couldn't hear what was happening, but I imagined the heavy thump of elderly feet descending the dark wood staircase that faced the front doors and the muttered curses of an old man rudely wakened from his slumber by someone senseless enough to be out in this weather. A silhouette appeared, shorter than I remembered, and a moment later the deadbolt thunked.

The door swung open, and Mrs. James stared up at me. She had her pleasant, grandmotherly face on as she squinted at me through her round-rimmed spectacles, but her expression shifted as she recognized me. Probably not by name, but the downturn of her wrinkled mouth and the furrowing of her brow told me she had identified me as not-a-tourist.

"Hello, Mrs. James," I said, and held out my right hand. She glared down at the tiny puddle forming as rainwater dripped off my sleeve onto her floor, and I pulled my hand back. "You probably don't remember me. Hazel Walsh. I lived in Fairbrook until about three years ago?"

Not a question. Speak with authority. Control your voice.

"Three years ago," I repeated more firmly.

"I heard you the first time," she said. "What do you want? We're closed for the season."

"I know, and I'm sorry to disturb you. My car broke down, and I wondered whether you might take me in for the night."

She chewed her lower lip. "You can pay?"

I considered reminding her of the inn's legendary hospitality to those in need, and thought better of it. My bank account could take the hit, though I'd never hear the end of it if I had to borrow from my parents later. "I can, thank you."

Mrs. James held the door open, and I stepped over the threshold. "You'll have to make up your own bed," she said, and locked the door behind me. "Got the arthritis in my fingers."

"I can do that."

She shuffled to the desk, a massive and heavy-looking affair that matched the decor of the rest of the inn: dark wood, stiff furniture, black and white photos framed on the walls. Smaller touches added during renovations in the seventies did nothing to make the place look less like something out of a horror movie. I set my bags on the emerald green diamond-patterned carpet.

Mrs. James shuffled through cards in a Rolodex behind the desk, then plucked a key off the wall and handed it to me.

"I hope I didn't wake your husband," I said.

She snorted. "I should hope not. He's been dead two years. Hate to see him come around now." She knocked on the wood of the desk, and I felt a small spark of superstitious camaraderie.

"I'm so sorry for your loss."

"I'm not." She motioned toward the staircase. "Third floor, hallway to your left, room 313. Linens in the closet right beside your room. No breakfast will be served."

Before I could request a different room number, she'd disappeared through a door next to the desk and locked the door behind her.

"Thanks," I mumbled, and headed up the stairs.

* * *

I'd expected to fall into a coma-like sleep as soon as my head hit the pillow. A heart-stopping fright, a white-knuckle drive, and a strange welcome back to town had exhausted me, but my brain wouldn't obey my commands to shut up and go to sleep. I left my room to scout for something to read from the collection of abandoned books that the Jameses kept as a constantly renewing lending library. Most people's vacation reads didn't appeal to me. Lots of romance, a bit of fantasy… same thing, really. Totally unrealistic. I preferred to keep my dreams of adventure and freedom grounded in reality. To my mind, sexy billionaire stalkers were no more real than dragons and ogres, and I'd dismissed both genres as a waste of time when I'd worked at the used bookstore in town. I glanced over the travel literature, memoirs, and mysteries, but found nothing I hadn't read before.

I trudged to my room empty-handed, careful to avoid the creaky bits of the stairs. It wasn't so much that I worried about waking Mrs. James—though that was a concern—but that the creaking seemed a lot more creepy and a lot less oogy-boogy hilarious than it had when the halls were filled with friends.

After an hour of tossing and turning (helpfully counted down by the ticking of the old-fashioned alarm clock on the bedside table), I got up again. *Might as well find something interesting to do.* My thoughts had become a jumble of unknowns, of shattered dreams and plans that would never come through, all of it sending my heart fluttering up into my throat. My brain was headed into Irrational Panic Land, and that was never a fun trip. I pulled my thick socks on, threw a black hoodie over my t-shirt, and pulled my mousy brown hair into a messy ponytail.

One distinct advantage of the off-season was the fact that I wouldn't have to worry about meeting the future love of my life as I roamed the halls in my pink polka-dot pyjama pants. Still, I took a minute to wash a dozen spots of acne mask off my chin and forehead. No need to frighten Mrs. James if she did come up.

The oldest section of the inn was the creepiest by far, so naturally I headed there. I've found that the best way to escape my semi-rational fears is to let myself get scared by something I know to be harmless, something I can let go of more easily than my anxieties. Like the spirits or monsters roaming these halls. Just a legend. A game.

And that little fairy girl... My stomach tightened. A coincidence that it happened here. *She was obviously off her rocker to begin with, poor thing.*

I tried a few of the numbered doors, interested to see what the older and more expensive rooms looked like inside, but all were locked tight. The only knob that turned belonged to a door with no number on it.

The door swung toward me on silent hinges, revealing a dark staircase heading up.

The attic. There had to be something interesting up there. My grandmother's attic had been full of weird old shit like mink shoulder wraps (complete with paws and faces) and rusted strap-on roller skates. The inn was bound to have even older stuff.

I hurried back to my room to grab the flashlight from my bag, then headed up the stairs. They creaked horribly under my feet. The musty air turned colder as I climbed, and I pulled my sweatshirt tighter.

My tiny light picked out dark shapes when I reached the top, none of them welcoming. A hulking, monstrous form to my left nearly made me retreat down the stairs, but it was only a mannequin with blankets tossed over it.

"Hush now, girl," I whispered, a soothing phrase my grandmother had used when I was a nervous child. She'd been more of a comfort to me than my own overbearing parents ever had, and was probably the only reason I was a remotely normal and functioning person. *God rest her soul.*

I moved around the perimeter of the massive attic, stepping from beam to beam in case the floor—or rather, the ceiling—wouldn't hold my weight. My physique rested somewhere in the middle of what my friend Lisa Flanker had once called the Waif-Whale

Spectrum. Healthy and normal, unless you were in movie-and-magazine world. Athletic enough to climb the ropes in gym class, but not nimble or dainty enough to take anything but the utmost care as I sneaked around a dark attic.

I found a string hanging down from the centre of the roof and gave it a tug. The light startled me. I hadn't expected it to work. Now the attic became something more interesting and less frightening, and my heartbeat slowed to normal as the light chased away the darkness.

A door to a partitioned-off area caught my eye, only because it looked so out of place. Everything else in the attic was covered in a thick layer of dust and cobwebs, but this door—dark polished wood carved with gorgeous floral patterns—was clean. I leaned closer and set my hand on the cut-glass knob, which didn't match the brass fittings on every other door in the inn. It seemed to vibrate briefly under my fingers, then stilled.

My mental exhaustion was obviously catching up with me. I turned the knob, but the door wouldn't open.

Go back to bed, I advised myself. But I still didn't feel sleepy. Just drained, bored, and not ready for a tomorrow full of disappointed glances from my mother—not to mention the "I told you so" looks from classmates who had never left the island.

I turned to the chests and boxes that lined the walls, searching their contents to distract myself. A tiny part of me feared finding the skeleton of a young child who had become trapped during a game of hide and seek decades before. Grandma always warned me and my cousins about that danger when we played at her house. The skeleton would still be wearing clothes, tattered with age and moth-eaten. Her eyes would stare up at me, empty sockets filled with—

I opened a chest, screamed, and let the lid slam shut as I stumbled back and fell onto my arse. *Shit, shit, shit. Oh God. Grandma was right. Fuck.*

I forced my breathing to be calm, and my mind soon followed. *That was not a dead child. Take another look.*

"I don't want to," I answered out loud, but crawled back to the round-topped chest, not trusting my trembling legs. My hands were faring no better, and I almost let the lid fall again before I hoisted it all the way open.

A doll stared up at me. A baby doll, but oversized. Its hard face was painted with what might once have been charming features, but time had not been kind to her. The doll's lips were brown, not the rosy pink I suspected they'd once been, with a cold tone to them that lent much to the impression of her being a dead child. Empty glass eyes stared up at me, unblinking, with spider-leg lashes painted around their perimeters. Her skin was white, save for a faded spot of orange on each cheek and a crooked lightning bolt crack that marred her from her hard-haired scalp to the middle of her left cheek.

I had no urge to touch her, but someone must have once loved this horrifying monster. Some little girl had thought her beautiful. And now she'd been discarded, closed away forever. I shuddered and reached up to close the chest.

As I did, the light from the bulb overhead caught a flash of something bright, nearly hidden beneath the doll's filthy skirt. A collection of jewellery, all jumbled in a box. Costume stuff, and probably worthless. I held my breath as I shifted the doll sideways and plucked out the tin box that had lost its lid somewhere along the years.

This was a much more pleasant find than the doll. A brooch caught my eye. Even in the dim light of the attic, the colours of the gems stood out bright and bold, forming the shape of a beautiful long-tailed bird. I reached into the box to scoop it up.

"Ouch!" I dropped the pin and shoved my bleeding finger into my mouth. Not a deep cut, but it stung badly. The faint, coppery taste of blood washed over my tongue.

Pretty, but not worth it, I decided, and hoped it hadn't given me tetanus in the bargain. I picked more carefully through the box. The only other thing that caught my eye wasn't a brooch or a necklace, but a key.

It wasn't made of metal, like the keys used by the hotel, but of glass or crystal, and felt unexpectedly heavy when I lifted it. It was about ten centimetres long, with only two teeth at the bottom. Nothing complicated, but the head of the key was certainly something. Formed in the shape of a skull, it grinned blankly up at me. I wrapped my fingers around the top, covering the toothy smile.

"Freaked out enough to sleep yet?" I asked myself, and opened my hand again. The key wasn't as creepy as the doll or as dangerous as the jewellery. In a way it was quite pretty. The overhead light cut through it and made the glass glow softly, and there was something appealing about its soft lines.

I stood and closed the chest, but kept the key in my hand. *It's not stealing if it doesn't leave the building,* I reasoned, and turned to head down to bed.

The pretty door caught my eye—the one with a different knob. Could the tall key slot match the skeleton key? I suspected the key was strictly for decoration, but tried it anyway.

The lock clicked and the door popped open toward me, showing a sliver of darkness beyond.

"Go to bed," I ordered myself, but didn't listen. Instead I pocketed the key, reached for my flashlight, and opened the door.

The beam refused to cut through the utter blackness beyond.

"Weird," I muttered. I stepped one foot in, following the rafter I'd been standing on, moving cautiously. The blackness didn't abate, and my flashlight didn't pick out any odd shapes. Not even walls.

I shone my flashlight upward and caught sight of a dangling string high overhead. Maybe out of reach. Maybe not.

I stepped forward to reach for it, and screamed as the floor disappeared and I plunged into darkness.

3

Sometimes falls come in slow motion, made up of seemingly endless moments of flails and stumbles and near-catches. Not this time. Just as I realized I was falling farther than I had any right to, I slammed into a hard surface. Cold stone scraped the knees of my pyjama pants, and I opened my eyes to bright lights. Not electric lights, but flickering flames—and that was the least unusual thing that surrounded me.

Voices filled the air, screaming or yelling, all speaking over each other so I couldn't tell what anyone was saying.

They sounded angry. My heart kicked into a gallop, and cold sweat covered my skin.

I curled instinctively into a ball to protect myself from the huge shapes gathered around me, but couldn't close my eyes. *Costumes,* I thought as I caught confused glimpses of furred legs and scaled hands. *Some kind of furry convention.*

Yeah. Here in Fairbrook. During the off-season. At the frigging Old Brook Inn, which you were the only person staying at. Look again.

"Kill her!" screamed a voice that sounded completely inhuman. A carnivorous voice. I raised my head from the floor and pushed up onto my stinging knees.

And then I screamed. I always hated screamers in books and movies, but for this I could forgive myself. A hulking creature—*troll,* I thought. *No, ogre*—stood in front of me with a massive axe raised high over its shoulders, ready to bring the blade down on my neck.

"Stop!" I yelled, holding out my hand as though that would stop the deadly blade from reaching me. The ogre hesitated, a confused look crossing the hideous brownish-green face that seemed to be all lower jaw, with protruding teeth and massive lips. Its beady eyes looked down at me, then to my left.

"Lieutenant," it said, "I don't think this is her."

"Finish it!" ordered that terrifying voice. I turned slowly and raised my other hand in surrender.

This is a horrible joke. It had to be. I glanced at the faces that made up the crowd, all standing too close for me to get a real handle on where I might be. I had fallen into a room of monsters. The ogre was the largest, but the others were no less fearsome. A man with the head of a bull. A centaur, dressed only in the blood that dripped over her shoulders and breasts. Things I didn't have words for and couldn't wrap my mind around.

Everyone turned to the creature giving orders. She stood like a human, and parts of her appeared to be. Her legs, hips, and torso were shaped like a woman's, but covered in a thick coat of spotted grey fur. A similarly furred tail with a black tip swung in agitated arcs behind her, matching her angry face, which resembled a silver leopard's. She wore thick rings in her ears, and sharp silver spikes pierced her face between her whiskers. Aside from the jewellery, the only thing she wore was a gore-spattered violet sash over one shoulder that crossed her chest and attached to her sword belt. Short-fingered hands gripped a curved sword.

I'm dreaming. I fell, I knocked myself out, and I'm dreaming. Hallucinating. I have a concussion.

There was no possibility any of this was real.

The cat woman stepped closer, and the knives strapped to her belt clinked together. "I said finish it! This is one of Verelle's tricks. Hold her."

"She's shifted!" someone bellowed. Strong hands grabbed my arms and forced them behind my back. I struggled, but it only made my shoulders scream with pain.

The ogre looked doubtful.

The cat woman snarled. "Then I'll do it. Major Zinian will hear about your failure, and he will not be pleased."

The ogre lowered its head and raised its axe again.

"Please," I begged, feeling half stupid for being so terrified when I knew none of this was real. But it all *felt* real, from the stone floor to the chill of the air, from the animal smells of sweat and fur to the suffocating tightness in my chest. I fought down panic that was as real as any I'd ever felt. "I don't know what a Verelle is, and I—"

"Shut up," the cat ordered, and grabbed my hair to force my head down. "You won't fool us. We know all of your tricks."

My body trembled. "I swear, I just opened a door, and I was here…"

Her low growl silenced me, save for a terrified sob I couldn't hold in.

"Stop."

A lower voice, more human. I only shook harder. With my head down, I couldn't see anything but the crowd of feet in front of me parting. I closed my eyes. Something cold touched my chin. Metallic. A blade. I pictured the cat's great, curved sword, and felt like vomiting as it lifted my chin.

"Look at me," the human voice ordered.

I forced my eyes open and was confronted by the strangest feet I'd ever seen. Human…ish. Longer toes than normal, with curved claws instead of toenails, and skin covered in tough blue scales to the knees. I didn't want to look higher, but the sword beneath my chin insisted. My gaze continued up the legs, which were covered by ragged pants from the knees up. Above that, hard abs and a chest that would have looked comfortingly human if not for the faint blue patina that shaded parts of the bronze skin, or the extra set of muscles under the otherwise highly acceptable pectorals. Spots of blood had dried on his skin. The fingers of the smooth hand that gripped the straight-bladed sword ended in sharp black claws. I let myself look up to the creature's broad shoulders, where massive, bat-like black wings arched high behind him. Dark scales dotted their bony parts in patches.

"Look at my eyes," he ordered, "or die now." The blade tilted sideways, a reminder of how easily he could follow through on the threat.

I swallowed hard, and the tip of the blade pricked again at my throat. Another deep breath, and I looked up.

I met his eyes, and they were enough to keep me from noticing anything else for several moments. Bright green, and blessedly normal. Not snake eyes, not feline slits for pupils. The thick black eyebrows that topped them furrowed, but seemed more intensely observant than angry.

"Please," I said again. "I don't know why I'm here."

His mouth twisted into a snarl, revealing long, white canine teeth. He turned toward the cat person, and I noted the deep scars that marred his right cheek. "It's not her."

When he returned his attention to me, his roughly cut black hair fell over his face. At least, the parts of it that weren't held behind the thick horns that spiralled back like bony corkscrews from his hairline.

Devil. That name came to me as easily as *centaur* had, but seemed not entirely right. As he glared down at me, I thought that it might be close enough. "Where is she?" he demanded.

"I don't know who you're talking about," I said, and forced my voice to be stronger. The others in the room had fallen silent, but I still barely heard myself. "I don't know where I am, or who any of you are, or what's going on. I just want to wake up or go home or do whatever will get me out of here. Please."

The cat person stepped closer. "Zinian, it's a trick. This may not be her, but Verelle was here moments ago, ready to fall under our blades. She disappeared, and this one came. She's human, and involved in this somehow. End her."

The devil man—Zinian—turned away and disappeared in the crowd. A crash echoed through the room, followed by the clatter of metal hitting the floor. He returned, jaw clenched, and looked down at me. "We'll do nothing until we find out what's happened here." He motioned for the ogre to come closer. "Lock her up and keep watch until I return. No one else is to see her. Understood?"

The ogre brightened. "The dungeons?"

Zinian frowned. "Lock her in Verelle's bedroom. I'll return as soon as I can. Jaid, come with me. All others, be about your business in the palace. Clean it out, top to bottom. By morning, this one should be the only human living."

My stomach lurched.

The cat woman fell in beside him, and the others dispersed. Before I could thank them for not killing me, the ogre hoisted me up. I cried out as I was hauled upward, then tried not to vomit as the creature's meaty shoulder hit me square in the stomach. It grunted and patted my ass, which I chose to believe was supposed to be a comforting gesture.

"I can walk!"

The ogre didn't listen. I flopped against its back as its uneven gait carried us on. At least this one wore clothing, a long tunic-style shirt with no sleeves. I caught the surprising scent of a mossy forest rising from the ogre's skin.

We passed into a dark room, and the ogre tossed me on a massive bed. I scrambled backward and off the far side, then scooted underneath. The ogre sighed. I watched its massive feet pass as it went to check the windows. The door closed behind it as it left me, and the wood creaked as the huge body settled against the other side.

Good at following orders, I thought. *Lucky for me he hesitated earlier.*

I left the safety of my hiding place and ran to the windows. There were several in the room, tall enough to almost reach the high ceiling. What they lacked was any visible mechanism for opening them. The night-dark streets far below me flickered with firelight. Ghastly shapes flew over the buildings of a city in the middle of a war. The windows were thick, but I still heard screams.

I backed away, heart hammering.

No light switch in here, and no one had left me a torch or a lamp. I'd dropped my flashlight when I fell. All I had was the skeleton key. I gripped it tight in my fist, squeezing so hard I expected to leave a skull-shaped impression on my palm.

It's not real, I reminded myself, even as I regretted not reading those fantasy books I thought were so silly. *I don't know where this is coming from, but it's a dream.*

I took a few deep breaths and looked around the room. I could hardly see anything in the faint light from the window. A wardrobe, bookcases, dressers and tables. Books. A few toys.

I didn't look closer, but retreated to the bed. On top, this time.

I pulled a blanket over me to fight the sudden chills that made me tremble. It was a more comfortable bed than the one at the inn, but I wanted nothing more than to wake and find myself resting on that old mattress and slightly lumpy pillow.

Even a hospital, if I actually did fall. *I hope someone finds me.*

A sigh and a grunt sounded from the other side of the door. For some reason, I felt better. The ogre seemed to be one of the few monsters here who didn't want me dead.

I expected that I wouldn't sleep, but soon my eyelids grew heavy.

Don't sleep. Don't.
Don't.

* * *

I opened my eyes to morning sunlight illuminating the room—and the most hideous face I'd ever encountered staring at me from the edge of the bed.

"Shit!" I yelled, and rolled backward, taking the blankets with me. I sailed off the far side of the bed, rolled up like a burrito in the silk sheets, then landed hard on the floor. The key hit the floor next to me, and I snatched it up.

The creature on the far side of the bed yelped and thudded toward the door. After a few moments of silence I fought my way free of the blankets and peered over the edge of the mattress. The ogre that had almost taken my head off the night before stood in the corner, twisting the hem of his shirt between his meaty, green fingers.

No, I realized as I looked closer. I was far from an expert on mythical creatures of any stripe, but something about its body shape, the quiet way the creature watched me, and the careful arrangement of the long hair that covered its scalp in thin patches made me think "he" was actually female. I just hadn't seen it the night before.

Best not to presume anything, I decided. Maybe they didn't care either way, or maybe saying the wrong thing would get me killed.

"Hello," I said.

The ogre glanced over at me, then looked down again. "I'm sorry I frightened you. I couldn't tell whether you were breathing, and Major Zinian told me to make sure you stayed safe."

"I was breathing," I said. "Not sure how safe I am." I slipped the key into my pocket and rubbed my thumb over the smooth skull. It was the closest thing I had to a rabbit's foot, and a comforting reminder of the sane world I'd left behind.

The ogre's heavy brows lifted, then furrowed, and it stepped closer, limping slightly. "You're safe. Everyone was screaming for your blood last night, but they won't go against Zinian's orders."

So a thin sort of safety. Not exactly a situation I felt comfortable with. "Zinian. He's the…" I trailed off, not knowing what to call him. Instead, I mimed spiralling horns coming from my head.

The ogre grinned, revealing huge, blunt teeth like sunken gravestones. Her bottom canines, strong and sharp, protruded from her mouth when it closed. "That's him. 'Amalgus' is the word you'd be looking for."

"Thank you." Not that it made me feel any better, but any detail about where I was granted me a step toward control. "And you are…"

"My name's Auphel. I'm an ogress."

"Awful?" I repeated, thinking I must have misheard.

"*Ow*-full," she said. "But that was a good try."

"Thanks for not killing me last night, Auphel."

The mottled skin of her cheeks deepened to a darker shade of green, and she pulled her upper lip in to chew on it. "I was supposed to. Major Zinian had such a solid plan, and I meant to do well. But then Verelle was gone, and you were there, and you didn't look like someone I was supposed to… I mean, you were human, and that's bad, but…" She shrugged. "Lieutenant Jaid was quite angry."

"The cat person?"

"Felid," she corrected. "And yes." Her tiny black eyes glistened.

"I'm sure it's fine," I said, and tried not to think too hard about the fact that I was comforting an ogre. *An ogre. This is insane. Why can't I be hallucinating something normal?* I squeezed the key tighter, then forced myself to let go of it. "You want to come sit over here?"

Auphel bit her thumb, then shuffled hesitantly over and sat on the end of the bed. It sank under her weight, and I climbed up to sit cross-legged near the pillows.

"Did you get hurt last night?" I asked, nodding at her leg.

She patted the limb she'd been limping on. "Old injury from early training days. I um… I don't like to talk about those times." She sounded about to cry.

"I'm sorry." An awkward silence followed. "You've done a good job protecting me," I added. "So that Zinian fellow should be pleased."

Auphel sighed, and her shoulders slumped. "I was supposed to be ready for this. Mama tried to say I was too small and girlish, but Zinian corscrupted me because he thought I could be a benefit to the rebellion."

I kept my expression neutral at the idea of this huge and well-muscled creature being considered too feminine for anything. I hated to imagine what a big male would look like.

Corscrupted, I noted. Not conscripted. A mistake I might have made when I was a child.

"How old are you, Auphel?"

"Old enough for a lot of things, I guess." Her nose wrinkled.

A lump formed in my throat. I'd been afraid of someone who now seemed young and friendly, and perhaps even scared of me. This monster hardly qualified for the title, as far as I could tell. To be fair, she'd had an axe over my neck, but I decided we could leave that in the past. Besides, she might be helpful when I needed to escape. *Assuming any of this is real.*

"Where are we?" I asked. "Not the building. This place."

"Elurien," she said, sounding surprised.

At least it sounds nice.

My stomach growled, and Auphel squinted at me. "You're hungry. I shouldn't leave, but…" She went to the door and looked out. "There's no one else. If I go get you something from the palace kitchens, you'll lock the door behind me and let me back in?" She gestured toward the door, which I now saw locked from inside the room with a simple deadbolt. "Zinian gave me the key, but my hands will be full."

"How will I know it's you?"

"I'll knock like this." She leaned over the wooden chest at the end of the bed and laid out a long series of thumps with no pattern to them at all. "See?"

"If you do that, I'll know it's you." Polite knocks would go unanswered, I decided.

"There's a toilet room through that door if you need it," she added, nodding to a sliding pocket door near the bed, and left. The space felt safer once I'd turned the lock.

I used the bathroom quickly—with great appreciation for the running water and flushing toilet, though I was disappointed by the lack of a bathtub— then stood in the middle of the floor and looked around the room. Verelle's room, whoever that was. The rug beneath my feet, which covered most of the floor, depicted images set out in concentric rings, each one its own scene. I crouched to look closer. The middle of the rug held the sun, burning bright and yellow, sending out wavy beams that touched the rings closest to it. The first and smallest circle showed a pair of pale hands cupped around the sun. The next showed the same figure several times over, in different scenes. A white-robed woman with flowing blonde hair, sometimes wearing a crown with tall spikes. She touched people, stood in crowds, lifted her hands over them. It was all very Children's Story Bible, or would have been if Jesus had been a blonde white lady.

The next ring showed more people, becoming violent. It seemed out of place in this peaceful room. The next had them battling a dizzying array of monsters. The blonde was there, larger than she'd been in the previous ring, but no more detailed. Angels flew overhead, also fighting the monsters.

The outer rings, where the sun's rays no longer reached, were filled with more monsters. I scanned my memory for the words. Centaur, harpy, ogre, goblin, troll, fairy, dragon, and many I couldn't identify. I spotted a unicorn running a man through with its horn, and a horse with four wings.

Though only depicted in carpet and not intricate tapestry, the images became clearer the longer I watched them. I stood and looked away. It had been lovely from a distance, and the craftsmanship was undoubtedly superior, but what I saw there made my stomach hurt.

These were the monsters who had surrounded me last night, and I felt certain that Verelle was that human woman.

So what's happening to the rest of the humans, if this is their city?

My throat tightened as I toyed again with the key. Never had I wanted to return to boring old Fairbrook so badly.

Couldn't have dreamt up one of those nice worlds, could you, Hazel? Nope. You had to invent Monster Murder Land. Fan-fuckin'-tastic. Well done. Really.

I went to a window, where a chess set was laid out on a small table. No, not chess, I realized as I looked closer. Something similar, but with squares of varying sizes as the playing field. The pieces on one side were humans, monsters on the other. They were like tiny stone gargoyles, but carved with the features of different creatures.

I turned to the books next, housed on tall, whitewashed bookcases that matched the rest of the room's furniture. Book collections are always a good way to learn about someone, and I'd snooped bookcases at parties back home the way some people snooped medicine cabinets. I opened a leather-bound volume at random, not expecting to be able to read it. I never could read print in dreams.

I traced my fingers down over the page and found that I understood the words before me, though the shapes of the letters were unfamiliar. My eyes travelled naturally from right to left, as the curved and dotted text seemed to indicate, and the meanings were as clear as if I were reading English.

And in those days the monsters roamed the land, living as animals, without understanding. The humans came among them, living in peace, sharing the words of the Mother.

I snapped the book closed. "Living in peace," I repeated. The words sounded right to me, but the movements of my tongue felt strange. I wasn't speaking English.

I opened the book again to a later page, and read again. *Beware the liar, the disrupter, who seems to come in peace. Beware the true monster, fair of face and black of heart, with words of honey and claws of poison.*

Pleasant, I added to myself, and shivered. A beautiful monster. I hadn't seen those yet, though the amalgus thing might have fit if he hadn't had blood on his skin and murder in his voice.

The door clicked open behind me, and I put the book back on the shelf. "Managed the key with full hands, or couldn't find food?" I called over my shoulder, then turned.

My heart sank. It wasn't Auphel who stood in the doorway, but Zinian.

4

I stepped back until the edges of the bookshelves dug into my spine. My mind went blank. Zinian made no move to come closer, but he closed and locked the door behind him. My heart pounded. The sword rested at his side today, but neither that nor the daylight made him any less terrifying. He wasn't as tall as I'd thought when I'd looked up at him from the floor. Maybe a little under six feet, if you didn't count those horns. They reminded me of a type of wild goat I'd seen at the zoo. *Markhor*, I remembered, and the information grounded me. *I'm dreaming. I put him together from stories and animals and... I don't know. Nightmares. He's not real.*

He'd cleaned up since the previous night, though he hadn't changed his clothes. Scratches and cuts marked his skin, but he had apparently come through the night just fine.

Zinian stepped further into the room. His shoulders were hunched forward, and he held his wings lower than he had in the heat of thwarted victory. He frowned, though not at me. At the room and its contents. His fingers rolled into fists that only did a mostly decent job of hiding his claws as he stopped in the middle of the carpet. He looked down and flexed his toes, digging his thick talons into the image of the sun.

I sidestepped clear of the bookshelf.

Zinian turned to me, and his expression sharpened as he stalked forward, muscles tense under his scarred skin.

"Please," I said, knowing how stupid and weak it sounded, but not knowing what else to offer. "I told you, I'm not—"

Though he stood close enough that I could have touched him, he ignored me. Instead, he reached up to take a delicate doll off the shelf next to my head. No terrifying baby doll, this. It was a woman, honey-haired and beautiful, with deep rose lips and bright blue eyes that sparkled over high-boned cheeks. She looked to be made of fine china, her white skin smooth and perfect. Her dress was petal pink and she wore a golden crown.

"Who is that?" I asked.

Zinian gripped the doll tight in his claws, tearing the delicate fabric. "Verelle," he said quietly. His voice sounded hollow, with a hint of an animal growl at the edges. "Queen and protector of the humans. Bane of monsters. Sorceress. It's a good likeness."

He held the doll up, letting sunlight glint in its long tresses. A strange expression crossed his face, something beyond rage. In one quick motion he placed his clawed thumb under the doll's pointed chin and snapped her head clean off. It fell to the floor and rolled under the bed, looking like a golden dust bunny.

He dropped the body and turned to me. I tried not to stare, but it was hard. He was so *other*. The human aspects of his appearance—his ruggedly masculine face shape, the well-formed torso and arms—only made the monstrous bits seem stranger. I focused on his eyes. Unnatural in their brightness, but something I could look at without feeling I was going crazy.

"Like what you see?"

I swallowed hard. "I just—I've never seen anyone like you before."

He snorted. "I get that a lot."

Arrogant in the bargain, I thought, but was far too frightened to offer a dismissive roll of my eyes. Instead, I gripped the key and reminded myself again that it was a dream.

And yet, in the light of day, it all seemed so real. Every detail was perfect, from the gentle whisper of his feet over the carpet to the faintly smoky smell he'd carried in with him.

"Who are you?" he asked.

"Hazel," I said. No one else here had offered last names.

"How was it done?" He spoke calmly, but I felt no less threatened. He stood too close to allow my nerves to settle.

"How—What?"

Excellent. Blow the enemy away with your wit and intelligence.

Zinian's lips tightened, hiding the fangs that were so easily visible when he spoke. "I knew when I looked in your eyes that you weren't her. She's never been able to hide herself from me quite that well, but few know what to look for. Jaid's instinct to kill you was a good one."

"Oh."

"But something happened. Everyone says the same thing, that they had Verelle cornered in her outer chamber, at their mercy. And then she was gone, and you were there. How was the exchange done, and what has she offered to make you take such a risk?" He tilted his head slightly, and his eyes softened. "Or what did she threaten you with?"

"I've never met her. I'm not from this world." The words came slowly, like my brain refused to believe they were necessary.

"You speak our tongue well enough."

"That's surprising to me, too."

His lip lifted in a silent snarl. "Magic."

He leaned in closer, and in spite of myself I looked away from his eyes. My gaze landed on his cheek, where four thin, jagged scars followed the line of his cheekbone. Well-healed claw marks, though I didn't know what would have dared attack him.

"Tell me where she is, and we'll see that you're well treated."

"I can't."

"She's gone. You don't have to fear her now."

I laughed nervously. "No, it's not that. I'm seriously not from here." I motioned to my pyjamas. "I haven't seen much human fashion in this place, but I doubt this is usual. Right?"

He frowned as he took in the scuffed knees and pink polka dots on my pants and the fuzzy slipper-socks that covered my feet. His gaze moved up over the black zip-up hoodie, which covered my upper curves and did a half-decent job taking the place of the bra I was now thinking I should have thrown on before I went exploring. His gaze lingered a little too long, and my face grew warm. It had been a while since anyone as attractive as him had given me that kind of a once-over.

Not attractive, Hazel. Monster. Devil. If I found that even remotely attractive, I definitely had a concussion.

"No," he acknowledged. "Your attire is most unusual." He crossed his arms. "You've had no contact with magic-workers?"

"Um... No? Well, besides a magician at my cousin's birthday party when she turned eight. And we played with a Ouija board this one time, but that..." I cleared my throat. "Not real magic. Not until last night, I guess. If that's what the key is."

My stomach clenched. *Not possible.* Magic was for silly books and fairy tales. I put my hand in my pocket and pinched my thigh hard. The sharp pain brought tears to my eyes, but did nothing to wake me up.

Zinian's hand went to his sword. "What are you doing?"

"Checking." I counted to five and forced myself to breathe calmly. "This is how I got here. Not some exchange of bodies. Not helping anyone escape." I pulled the key from my pocket and held it close to my body. High-pitched panic flooded my veins when he plucked it from my hand. My chest tightened. "That's mine."

He arched a dark eyebrow. "I know." He lifted it, testing its weight, and examined it in the light of the window.

"I used it to open a door in an attic," I explained. "I stepped through, and fell."

Zinian said nothing to that.

My mouth went dry. "Can I have it back, please?"

"There are others who will need to see this."

"But it's not yours." I felt like a child, whining about fairness and not wanting to share. But if I chose to accept that this was really happening, that key was my only hope of getting home.

He nodded. "I'll see that you get your key as soon as we determine that it's not dangerous. I know little about magic other than recognizing its presence, but there are others who will be able to tell us about where it might lead."

"Fairbrook," I said, almost under my breath. It didn't matter. I cleared my throat. "That's fine," I added, knowing there was no point trying to wrestle it away from a monster with a sword. *An amalgus with a sword,* I corrected myself. The name was easy to remember. He was as much an amalgamation of random shit as he was a creature in his own right.

He pocketed the key and paced the perimeter of the room. He moved with more grace than I'd expected after seeing him the night before. But he'd been exhausted then. And probably stiff from all that killing.

"Is Auphel coming back?" I asked. "She was bringing food."

"The kitchens had already been raided. She might be a while." He continued to pace.

"Oh. Did you need anything else from me, then?" I wanted him gone. He reminded me of a caged lion, and I didn't care for being trapped with him.

He looked over his shoulder at me, a maneuver that required shifting one wing aside. "I suppose not. We'll have to decide what to do with you, of course, but I think General Grys will accept my assessment of you."

I swallowed a lump in my throat. "Which is what?"

"That you're a victim here. Verelle somehow called you to take her place and went somewhere else. Those who understand magic better may find a way to track her down." He walked to the bookcase and the doll's body crunched under his bare foot, shattering into sharp pieces that didn't seem to bother his scaled feet.

"So this isn't over for you?"

His lips curved in a dark smile that didn't reach his eyes. "Until I see her head roll, it's not over."

The room was quiet. Even the streets outside had calmed since the previous night.

"What did she—" I began, and stopped. It might be too personal a question, given his obvious hate for her, and I didn't want to get on his bad side. On the other hand, I didn't know when I'd be getting home, and needed to know what the hell was going on. I forced my way past my nerves. "What happened last night?"

Zinian grimaced. "You joined us at a bad time."

"But you won, right?"

"Bad for humans," he clarified. "Which you are, correct?"

I remembered the order he'd given the night before. *By morning, this one should be the only human living.* Were the rest dead, whoever they had been? My knees trembled. I forced them to hold me up, though collapsing to the floor and begging for mercy seemed like a valid option. "I am. I'm not a part of whatever is happening here, though, I swear."

He narrowed his eyes at me, not unkindly. "You can relax. I have no desire to see you harmed, and I hope for your sake that you can return home. This is not a good time or place to be human." His mouth quirked in a rueful smile. "It's not even a good place for those who resemble humans."

I took in his blue-bronze skin, wings, and heavy-looking horns, and wondered how that could possibly be a problem for him. But then I remembered Auphel, the felid Jaid, and the strange crowd from the previous night, and understood that to them, he probably appeared to be very human. It was all a matter of perspective.

"They all seem to respect you," I said. When he turned to me, I quickly added, "Not that I think you look human. I just thought you meant that—"

"It's fine." He almost smiled, but not quite. "The fact is that my appearance is a liability. I've only come as far as I have because my skills and knowledge have been vital to us reaching Verelle after hundreds of years of trying." He shrugged. "So while my instinct is to hate you for what you are, as any monster would, I have a certain sympathy for your position. It won't be an easy one."

It seemed the word monster wasn't an insult here as it was at home. Perhaps he was using another word, and this was the only way my mind could translate it.

So we're accepting that this is real? I asked myself.

On a provisional basis, I answered. *Err on the side of caution.*

"I'd actually like to keep that key," I said, forcing my voice to keep steady.

Zinian reached into his pocket, but didn't return my property. "As I said, you'll have it soon enough." He went to the windows and looked out at the city below. "I should get out there. Would you care to see exactly what kind of world you've come into?"

My heart skipped. I really didn't want to. I wanted to get back in bed and sleep until I woke up at home. But if I was going to move forward as though this were actually happening, the first step to finding control and making a plan was to gather information. I would feel lost until I oriented myself.

"Can I dress first?"

He nodded toward the wardrobe. "Take what you wish."

I opened the white doors, which were painted in pale florals. The wardrobe was filled to bursting with clothes. Long dresses, mostly. Not tailored and fitted, but flowing and comfortable-looking. Kind of hippie-ish. I'd thought these fantasy settings were all about the corsets, and couldn't say I felt disappointed. The loose fit would work in my favour if this Verelle had been as dainty as the doll indicated.

I slid out the long drawer at the bottom of the wardrobe, and turned to Zinian. "This is a joke, right?"

He shook his head.

I'd expected shoes, but not like these. Six pairs of boots filled the space, all of them heavy, with vicious iron spikes studding the leather from the toes up to the ankle, covering the foot. Some of them had additional spikes dotting the leather up to knee-height or covering the bottoms of the soles.

Kinky.

"How does a person even walk in these?"

Zinian stepped closer. His shoulders tensed as he approached and his wings spread slightly, like the hackles rising on a dog. "It's all humans wear," he said quietly. "Good for kicking disobedient servants and slaves, and a visual reminder of who rules this world. Or who did, until last night."

I shuddered. "That's horrid."

"I'm so glad you think so." He returned to the bed and found a pair of golden slippers beneath it. "See if these fit you. They were only for wearing in her chambers, not in the streets, but I think they'd suit you better."

"Thanks."

The slippers were small, but the fabric had some give to it. Though they wouldn't offer much protection, they would have to be enough. I wanted nothing to do with those boots.

Zinian turned away as I slipped into a pale blue tunic-style dress. It trailed on the ground but didn't squeeze too badly, except across the bust. I resisted the urge to throw my hoodie back on to cover myself.

"We'll have to see about getting you something more practical," he said as he looked me over. "We might be short on tailors for a while, but someone should be able to make you something less…. Well." He cleared his throat and offered me his arm. I appreciated the gesture, but realized he was probably keeping me close for everyone else's safety as much as mine.

Less what? Human? I glanced down. The dress didn't do as much for my figure as some, but it did cling to some rather feminine spots. Practical would be better.

As we walked through the gleaming white stone halls of the massive palace (filled with enough airy tapestries, sculpted furniture pieces, and sparkling windows to satisfy any fairy tale princess), the other monsters we passed nodded respectfully to Zinian. I got a few glares, raised lips, and bared fangs, but all in silence. Distaste. Not threats. Still, I clung a little tighter to my terrifying protector.

These are the good guys, I reminded myself, remembering the terrible spikes on the queen's boots.

Then we stepped through massive double doors into the streets, and suddenly I wasn't so certain which side I'd got myself wrapped up with.

5

The fact that I'd missed the action was only a small mercy.

I stayed close to Zinian, who was at least familiar even if I still wasn't completely sure I could trust him, and kept my gaze trained on the cobblestone street ahead of me. I'd have to look up some time, become familiar with the incredible variety of faces and bodies we passed, but knew that if I raised my eyes now I would be unable to stop staring. They'd hate that. Anyone would.

A high-sided cart passed, pulled by a pair of minotaurs. I peered inside. Bodies. Human bodies, piled on top of each other in a heap, limbs flopping over the sides. I gagged at the sight, and at the smell of blood rising from the corpses. Not a movie set. Not a dream. This, like nothing else, convinced me that all of this was real.

My stomach somersaulted, and I pressed a hand to my mouth to hold back the stinging bile that rose in my throat. My breath grew shallow, and I gripped Zinian's arm tight as I fought against the feeling I was about to faint.

He looked down at me. "Horrible, isn't it?"

I turned away as an ogre nearly twice the size of Auphel and with a far less pleasant personal odour scooped a young woman's body out of the gutter and tossed her onto a passing cart. I squeezed my eyes closed and took a deep breath that only filled my nose with the stench of death. "Horrible doesn't begin to cover it. Why?"

"Why did this happen? That's a question with a complicated answer."

I released his arm. "You led them, though? You did this?"

His brow furrowed. "General Grys is in charge of everything, but I played my part. I provided information that allowed us to defeat the magical protections around the palace that have made a monster uprising impossible for so long. So yes, in a way I did."

I turned toward a scraping noise approaching us from behind, and lost my fight against the urge to stare. The creature, which hurried toward us with a shuffling gate and a determined glare, looked like every bone in its body had been broken and poorly set. It opened a mouth filled with broken-off fangs, and reached its twisted hands toward me.

Zinian shoved me against a wall and spun on the creature, spreading his wings to shield me.

"Move along," he ordered.

A wheezing laugh. "Protecting a human. I knew I hadn't judged you wrong." The rasping voice dripped with disdain.

I pressed myself against the wall and wished Zinian had offered me a weapon to go with my new clothes. Something that would at least give me a fighting chance.

The muscles of Zinian's back shifted as he spread his arms. He hadn't drawn his sword. "She's not one of them. This isn't her fight."

"They're all the same."

I peered from beneath Zinian's wing and saw one bent and broken foot step forward. In an instant, Zinian had drawn his sword. "Your orders have nothing to do with her." He spoke as calmly as he had before. "Move on."

"Or you'll report me to Grys?"

"Or we'll deal with this here and now."

The street had fallen silent, and I imagined that all of the monsters had stopped to watch the scene play out. I hated that they were seeing me hiding, but knew there was nothing else I could do. Those horrible hands could have snapped me in half.

The creature let out a low growl and shuffled away. Zinian sheathed his sword and turned to me.

"Are you hurt?"

"No." I'd hit the wall hard, but the pain in my shoulder was nothing compared to being torn apart by my worst nightmare. I wasn't about to complain.

"Good. Stay close. We'll head back soon." He offered his arm again, and this time he added the protection of one wing held out, shielding me from curious glances from behind. The gesture, odd as it was, made me feel more relaxed. He was a strange guardian, and I didn't exactly feel comfortable walking with a monster, but I didn't doubt that I was safe with him.

We passed another human body. A man, bent backward nearly in half, spine snapped.

"Did they really deserve this?" The words were out before I could second-guess them.

I looked up to find Zinian's face a hard mask, showing no emotion as he watched the cleanup. "Humans have tortured us for centuries, ripping us from our mothers' arms, killing our children as punishment for parents' minor crimes, chaining us and humiliating us. Even those of us with a measure of freedom have lived in fear of the day when they would come and demand our service. At least we were merciful enough to let them die quickly when we finally came for them. It's better than they deserved."

And that's what I am to them, I realized. I shuddered. No wonder they glared. No wonder I needed a bodyguard.

We rounded a corner and found a handful of pink-skinned creatures of basically human shape, less than half my height, gathered around a heap of human belongings. Their faces ranged from long and thin-nosed to snub-featured, and their bodies from strong to gaunt. They each used one hand to shield their faces from the sunlight as they dug gleefully through the pile, pulling out metals and jewels and anything made of stone, squealing over their finds. They burrowed into the ever-growing pile, which other monsters added to as they cleared out the whitewashed cottages that lined the street.

"Welcome back, pretties!" one of the scavengers exclaimed, and planted a loud kiss on a golden coin.

A centaur who had been dumping a load of clothing on the pile reached down and snatched the coin. "Those will be ours," he said in a resonant voice, and crossed his arms over his broad chest. As Zinian and I crossed the street and moved around them, I noted that his human skin—which matched the chestnut colour of his horse-hide—was crisscrossed with long, deep scars.

The little creature leapt up, but the centaur held the coin well out of reach. "Gold and gems belong to the gaublings!" squealed the smaller creature. "They come from underground. You can take their grasses and wood, forest-dweller."

The centaur snorted. "My people mined this gold. If it belongs to anyone, it's us."

The imp-like creature—the gaubling, I supposed—snarled. "We'll see what General Grys says about it." He dove into the rubbish pile without his prize.

The centaur turned to us. "Major," he said, and looked at the coin somewhat sheepishly. "We have permission to take what the humans stole from us."

"And what good will gold do you?" Zinian asked, sounding more curious than accusatory. "Will it bring back those you lost below-ground? Return your sweat and blood to you?"

The centaur clenched his teeth, hardening the muscles of his heavy jaw.

Zinian turned away without an answer, and we continued our journey.

"Do humans in your world use coin?" he asked.

"We do. Gold like that would be worth a lot, I guess."

He nodded. "We don't. Monsters, I mean. We've always bartered with each other, even between species. Material things only have value because they're beautiful or useful." He stopped and sank onto a wooden bench with roses climbing its sides, narrowly avoiding stepping in a puddle of dark blood.

"This is what I feared," he said, obviously not speaking to me anymore.

"What?"

He hesitated, then seemed to decide I could be trusted with an answer. "Repeating their mistakes. Becoming greedy. Fighting each other. How long until a monster species takes the humans' place, believing themselves above everyone else?"

I didn't know what to say to that, but he seemed to want an answer. "I don't think I can offer advice on peace," I said. "Humans in my world treat each other horribly. We're not all bad as individuals, but…" I shrugged. "They say power corrupts, and I guess that's usually true. Maybe you all can do better."

Zinian nodded sadly. "I hope so."

"Did he say that the centaurs worked underground?" I tried to imagine that huge creature in those surroundings, and couldn't picture it.

Zinian's shoulders and wings slumped as he leaned forward. "That's correct. The captured gaublings were thrown in crates and shipped to the farmlands to work the soil and climb the fruit trees, while the centaurs were taken from their bright forests and forced to work in the cramped mines, hauling coal and diamonds and gold."

"That seems inefficient." I felt like I was missing something. "They would be stronger workers in their own habitats, wouldn't they?"

He shrugged. "Efficiency wasn't the goal. Centaurs working farms might have stayed strong and healthy, and possibly unmanageable. Gaublings working underground would have had the upper hand if they decided to free themselves. So the humans stuffed the creatures of air and sunlight into the dark mines, and put the gaublings out to be blinded and burned by the sun." He nodded at a pink head that poked out of the heap. "They should be white as snow. They should never have to see the surface."

My stomach clenched. "So they were easier to control when they were miserable?"

"And weak," Zinian added. "I have great respect for all of them for finding the strength to join us." He narrowed his eyes at me, taking me in. "It's refreshing to meet a human who doesn't follow the usual ways of thinking. Gives one a glimmer of hope that perhaps things can change for the better."

Before I could answer, Jaid approached. Her feline tail twitched excitedly, and her grin revealed long, yellow fangs.

"Lieutenant," Zinian said. "Tell me you bring good news."

"I do." She shot me a glare, then returned her attention to Zinian. "Come with me. This should please you."

We followed, though I had trouble keeping up with their long strides. The flowing skirt of my dress kept tangling up in my legs, and stones and rubbish bit at my feet through the soles of the golden slippers. Still, I didn't let myself fall behind, and we soon reached an open square lined with shops. The clearing out of human culture was continuing here, but at least the bodies had already been taken away.

A crowd had gathered, and Jaid cleared a path through it for us. In the centre of the square knelt a creature more human in appearance than any I'd seen living so far. A beautiful man, fair-haired, with skin that glowed from within. Wings sprouted from between his shoulder blades, massive and powerful, covered in bright white feathers.

An angel, I thought, and immediately felt stupid. He wasn't an angel any more than Zinian was a demon. Still, the name fit.

The creature held his head high even as he knelt in the mud, unmoving. He didn't object to the situation, or even seem aware of what was happening. Not drugged… just not there.

Jaid stalked forward and took the largest sword I'd ever seen from a half-man, half-deer creature who struggled under its weight.

"Watch," she said to Zinian. The crowd fell silent. No one asked for last words from the prisoner. Jaid raised the sword and brought it down through the back of his neck, just as Auphel was supposed to do to me last night with her axe.

I clapped my hands over my mouth to hold in a scream, but couldn't look away. I expected blood. Instead, the angelic figure collapsed, then disappeared. All he left behind was a handful of feathers.

Jaid turned to Zinian with a wild grin. "You see? She's well and truly gone. We are free!"

Zinian smiled, but it seemed forced. The rest of the crowd erupted into cheers, tears, and embraces. I stuck close under the shelter of Zinian's outstretched wing, not wanting to be trampled by the others as we moved toward the space the angel had occupied.

"What of these?" he asked, and scooped up a long primary feather. He twirled it between his fingers. "And what of the fact that we're still killing them? Yes, they're disappearing when they die. They're easy to catch now that she's not directing their actions. But they should have disappeared immediately if Verelle is dead." He caught another feather beneath his foot and ground it into the dirt. "How certain are we?"

Jaid rolled her eyes and patted Zinian's arm with one blunt-fingered hand. Her feline face was surprisingly expressive. "You're still in shock," she said softly. "We have our victory. I'm sorry you didn't get to kill her yourself, but it's over. Have a drink or ten, sleep it off. Then celebrate with us. You've earned it."

Zinian grunted. "I should take Hazel back to the palace."

The whiskers above one of Jaid's yellow eyes twitched. "Of course. Do join us when you're free." Her tone had turned icy, and I suspected it had everything to do with me.

"Not everyone is going to accept me as easily as you have, are they?" I asked as I hurried again to keep up. Zinian slowed as we got away from the crowd. He still held the feather in one hand.

"No," he said. "And the sooner you understand that, the better. Try to keep to yourself until we figure out what to do with you."

"Understood." I wasn't about to head out into the streets—or the palace halls, for that matter—without protection.

He didn't say anything else as we entered the palace, which felt clean and protective after the mess and violence of the streets. When we arrived back at my assigned room, Auphel was waiting. She rose from where she sat on the floor.

"I found food," she said, gesturing to a plate of roughly chopped root vegetables, all raw, and a chunk of bread. "I had to go to the garden to find anything good. Did you eat already?"

"I'd forgotten all about eating," I said, but my stomach quickly reminded me that bloody streets outside or no, I hadn't eaten in far too long. "Thank you so much." I snatched up the bread.

Zinian nodded and tossed the room key to Auphel, then left us.

"You gave him that?" I asked between mouthfuls, gesturing to the key. The bread was stale, but I ate all of it, then started on a chunk of carrot.

"He gave me an order," she said. "I'm glad he didn't hurt you."

Her grotesque face was a strangely comforting sight. Completely out of place in the well-appointed bedroom, but more pleasant than anything else there. She seemed to have a simple mind, but a kind one, and I was glad to have her guarding me.

We passed the day together. I offered to read to her from the books on the shelves, but we quickly found that human stories weren't the sort of thing a monster wanted to hear.

"Their stories are bad," Auphel observed. "I never liked talk of the spark, either." She scooped the doll head up off the floor and fiddled with the knotted hair. "I wish there was more to do here."

"What's the spark?"

She looked up, surprised. "I thought all humans knew about it. Don't you have it?"

I shrugged. "You tell me."

Her beady eyes widened. "It's the oldest story. When Maela, the Mother of all, created the world, she gave humans the spark. It's what makes them special. Makes them wise and able to do things that aren't natural."

"Magic?" I asked.

"That's supposed to be part of it, though I can't say I ever met any humans with real magic. But they say they all have it. Verelle had more of it, of course, and that's why she was queen for hundreds of years. It's how she made her flying soldiers, the ones that fought us and protected the humans for so long. She had the biggest spark, and the most magic." Auphel frowned. "The humans said that put her closest to the Mother."

"And monsters don't have... spark?"

"That's what the stories say, the ones that come from back when the Mother spoke to people."

My stomach clenched. "I see." Religion had never been my favourite topic. My mother called my beliefs wishy-washy, while a few of my college friends laughed at me for believing in anything beyond what they could see and touch. I considered my beliefs open-minded and reasonable, if flexible enough that Grandma would have beaten me with a Bible if we'd ever talked about them.

"This spark doesn't justify anyone hurting you, though," I said, remembering what Zinian had told me about the humans. "Even if it's true."

Auphel wiped her nose on her wrist. "Humans seem to think it does. Like they own the whole world. You want to talk about something else?"

We spent a few hours trading information about our worlds. My stories about cars and airplanes and printing presses were met with stark disbelief until Auphel decided that we had strong spark there, magic that allowed all of it. "You should keep quiet about that," she whispered, though no one was there to overhear. "Don't want anyone thinking you're the next Verelle, after all."

"I didn't make any of it," I whispered back.

She shook her head. "Don't risk it."

"Good. Thanks."

Auphel left me to get supper and brought me more bread, along with a slightly underripe tomato. I ate all of it, and she went back to the garden to find more. She returned with a pair of apples. "Found the orchard," she explained. "Had to break down a door."

After sunset, firelight lit the room from outside.

"They're burning human stuff they don't want to keep," Auphel explained before I could ask. "Celebrating."

I sat near the window and moved not-chess pieces around the board at random. "You know how to play this?" I asked. Auphel shook her head.

Someone screamed outside. It sounded human. My throat tightened.

Auphel's lips narrowed, and she motioned for me to come closer to her. She pulled back the blankets on the big bed, and I climbed in. "You don't need to hear that," she said.

"I thought the humans were all dead."

She sighed. "I suppose some will have been hiding. You're safe here, I promise."

That wasn't my concern.

I couldn't get a handle on anything. The monsters were free. The humans had been cruel and controlling. But the death, the destruction… these weren't good things, and never would be. Someone out there was afraid, maybe in pain, and at that moment I didn't care what they'd done to deserve it.

So much for quick deaths. A tear slipped from my eye. I wondered whether Zinian was out there following Jaid's suggestion that he have some fun, and tried not to imagine what he had done to enemies with those claws, those teeth, that sword.

"Oh, don't cry," Auphel said, sounding genuinely upset. "It's just… It's war, you know? It's a bad thing. But it will be over soon. At last. Just promise you won't try to go out there. You can't stop any of this."

That only made it worse. Self-pity quickly joined the party, and I didn't bother to shut it out. I'd landed on my feet as much as was possible in this world. I still had my head, thanks to poor Auphel being too kind to kill a stranger. But quite frankly, things had gone to shit since I had decided to explore that attic. I wanted to go home.

Auphel sat on the bed and stroked my hair. "Don't feel sad."

Another scream rang out. Auphel cleared her throat and hummed a few notes. The humming turned into a song. A lullaby. Her voice was as simple and sweet as her nature, a stark contrast to the thick and heavy tones of her speech. I found myself relaxing as she drowned out the noise of the streets.

"Thank you, Auphel," I said.

She patted my shoulder—or rather thumped it, and hard. "I'll take care of you."

"Where will you sleep?" I asked. "There's room on the bed."

"I'll sleep by the hearth," she said. "I'm not comfortable with these human things."

She stopped frequently to yawn, but kept singing until I felt myself drifting off.

This world needs more people like you, I thought. At least there was one monster I knew I could trust.

6

I woke with a plan. Not a grand plan for my life, and not the hourly breakdown that usually gave me a sense of control when everything became unmanageable. But it was a starting point, and that was all I needed.

I would take Zinian's advice and keep to myself. It might not be exciting, but Auphel would keep me company, and maybe I'd read some of those books to learn more about the conflict from those who could no longer speak. I knew better than to think the humans were undeserving victims, or that the monsters were paragons of virtue. There couldn't possibly be a perfect resolution in a situation like this.

But I wanted to understand.

Zinian had said there were monsters around who knew about magic. I hoped they'd be able to get me home. I could bide my time until then, perhaps make myself useful in a quiet way. I didn't like the feeling that Auphel was waiting on me as much as guarding me, and wondered whether I might be allowed to prepare my own food.

More responsibility for myself was the key. More control. It would make everything so much less frightening, and I was beyond ready to get rid of the tight, fluttery feeling in my chest.

I lay in bed for a while, listening to Auphel's gentle snoring. She was looking out for me. I wondered whether she needed the same from me, and whether I was in any position to offer my help. The poor ogress seemed so innocent and dangerously eager to follow orders. The thought of what she could be turned into saddened me.

But the war is over. Maybe she'll be free to go home now. I hoped she'd stay until I left, at least. I'd miss her.

I got up and did my morning stretches as quietly as I could. Auphel roused herself and rubbed the sleep from her eyes. "You do training exercises, too?"

"Not exactly. Just… physical conditioning, I guess. Staying limber."

She nodded and watched, then tried to copy my head-down position. She crashed to the floor and snorted. "I might stick with strength training."

"Maybe you just need to work on it," I said, laughing. "We could help each other. I'm so weak. How do you manage to carry that axe you had the other night?"

She grinned and opened her mouth to speak, but a knock at the door interrupted her. She hoisted herself off the floor and answered, using her broad form to block the entrance as she held the door firmly against anyone who might try to invade. She spoke quietly, nodded, and closed the door again.

"You should change," she said, nodding at the rumpled dress I hadn't taken off the night before. "They're deciding what to do with you. You might want to be there."

I dug quickly through the closet and threw on a brown dress, tying a thick ribbon around my waist with fumbling fingers, and dashed out the door. Auphel locked it behind us, then led the way down a spiral staircase and along a darker corridor than the ones I'd seen the day before. At the end we came to a huge wooden door that Auphel threw open without knocking.

It led to a conference room of sorts, containing a massive, round table made of stone. Auphel paused as a dozen faces at the table turned toward her. Some of the room's occupants already had hands or paws on their weapons, but relaxed when they saw her. Their irritated scowls remained, though. Zinian sat with his hands clasped on the table, unconcerned.

"What's she doing here?"

I turned toward the gruff voice. It took a moment for my brain to process what I was seeing. He was shaped like a man, and yet not. In fact, his shape changed slightly with each moment that passed. He had facial features, but they kept shifting, as though he was more of an indistinct idea than anything real. One moment he seemed to be made of smoke, the next of tar, the next of liquid grey stone. He was solid enough, though, which he proved when he slammed his fist on the table.

"Auphel!"

Auphel jumped. "General Grys, I was told that there was a meeting about the uh… prisoner."

Grys narrowed his glowing yellow eyes—the only constant feature in his face. "There is. I want to know why she's here. Who told you?"

"I—I thought I was supposed to…" Auphel's words trailed off, but she didn't back down. "Shouldn't she be here if you're talking about her?"

I looked around the table. Jaid was there, seated next to Zinian, and looking none too pleased. I recognized the massive ogre to her right as the one I'd seen in the streets the day before. He bore fresh scratches on his face, which made Auphel's look positively cherubic in comparison. He leered at her.

The others were an assortment of creatures, a collection of fur and scales and wings and horns that overwhelmed me. I turned to Zinian, the only semi-welcoming face.

"She should have a say in her fate, if she's here anyway," he said. I understood then who had sent the messenger. Auphel knew, too, I realized. But she wouldn't give him away, not even to the higher-ranking general.

Zinian stood. "Hazel, would you like to sit?"

"I'll stand, if it's all the same," I said. I had no desire to be near Jaid's claws or the glaring eyes of the strange bird woman who sat on Zinian's other side. He nodded and sat.

"We're sending you to an outlying human village," Grys said. He stared hard at me, as though daring me to refuse. Glad as I was to learn there were human settlements that hadn't been wiped out during the battles, I knew I couldn't go. "You'll be safer there," he added. "You'll leave tonight, and be among your own people."

He didn't have to add, *People who don't hate you.* I understood.

"It's the best thing," Jaid said. She spoke to Grys, not to me. "The city is ours now. A face like hers will never be accepted among us."

Zinian cleared his throat. "That's what they said about me."

Grys waved that off. "Your human aspects have always disturbed some, and your associations didn't help. But you're a monster. A proper one, if an unsettling one."

I'd have laughed at that if I hadn't been so frightened. True, I'd thought him unsettling at first, but he now seemed far less so than anyone else, at least in physical appearance.

Zinian tapped a claw on the table. "My point is that we prove ourselves by our deeds, not our appearance or our birth. She has no more to do with the humans here than you. Less than any of us, in fact. I say she should choose where she goes."

"Thank you," I said, too quietly for anyone to hear, but Zinian nodded.

Jaid turned to me. "You object to being sent to safety?"

"Yes, actually." I clasped my hands behind my back to keep them from trembling. *Stand up for yourself.* "Zinian told you about the key?"

Grys nodded. "We've learned nothing further from it."

"I'd like to be here if you do. I'm as eager to go home as you are to be rid of me. That key is my only chance, as far as I can tell."

"We've completed our investigations. You might as well take it," Grys said. He narrowed his eyes. "Try your key for a day or two. You'll report to us if you learn anything. If you don't, be prepared to move to the villages. One way or another, you'll be leaving the city."

"Thank you." It wasn't much, but maybe a few days would be enough time to find my way home. I felt certain that if my door was anywhere, it would be here in Verelle's city. If she had the most magic, surely her city did, too. Going elsewhere would doom me to staying in Elurien forever.

Jaid scowled. "We can't entrust magical objects to humans."

"Hazel's the one who used it before," Zinian replied. "I still think another door might help us find Verelle. If Hazel can open one—"

"Let it go," Jaid growled, but without real anger. "Verelle is gone. Be content with that."

The ogre leaned back in his chair. It creaked under the strain. "If that's settled…"

Grys turned to him. "I suppose it is, for now."

The ogre cracked his knuckles so loudly that it sounded like boards breaking. "Auphel should be returned to regular duties if the human is no longer a prisoner. I'd be happy to take her in as part of the rearrangement crew. We could use her strength."

Auphel stiffened beside me, fists clenched, but said nothing. She would do as she was told, though the idea of going with this creature obviously distressed her.

I couldn't blame her if she was afraid. He was practically salivating.

"I need Auphel to stay with me a while longer," I said. I knew I was far overstepping my rights, but she'd protected me. I had to return the favour. "She's helping me figure things out here, keeping me out of trouble. I won't be a bother to any of you if she's with me."

Jaid lifted her lips in a silent snarl. "The new human wishes to have a monster servant. How shocking. This is a bad idea, Grys."

"Not a servant," I added, before he could respond. "A friend. I understand it would be inconvenient to lose her for other purposes, but I do think this would benefit everyone." *Auphel more than most,* I added silently as I caught the disappointed scowl that crossed the male ogre's face.

"Having a monster with her to keep an eye on Hazel isn't a bad idea," Zinian said. "We believe her to be trustworthy, but having Auphel with her would allow us more certainty."

Grys waved an indistinct hand at us, then tossed the skeleton key onto the table. It skittered toward me, and I caught it from the air as it sailed off the end. "Go, then. Zinian, you'll continue to supervise."

Zinian nodded, and Auphel dragged me out of the room.

"That was pleasant," I said under my breath. I was still quaking inside from my unaccustomed display of nerve, but I felt stronger. More in control than I had since my arrival.

"It really was not." She shuddered. "I guess we're free now, though. Want to get some fresh air?"

My stomach turned at the thought of returning to the streets, but if I was going to find my way home, I'd need to explore the city. And I knew no one would dare mess with Auphel. "Definitely."

After a few wrong turns, we found the palace entrance. We stepped out into an empty street, though I heard voices from farther away. The sun beat down hard and hot as we walked, and I kept my eyes open for doors that looked as out of place as the one in the attic had.

"Thank you for asking to keep me," Auphel said as we headed toward the square. "I wouldn't want to work for Kringus."

I was about to respond, but the words disappeared as we rounded a corner and I stepped into a puddle.

Not water, but thick, dark blood. I gasped and jumped to the other side, and Auphel pulled me away. She put her body between me and the spiked boot on the other side of the puddle.

I turned away, but not before I saw the thin, shapely leg sticking out of it, torn off at the knee. I gagged, and spots appeared in front of my eyes.

"I'm sorry, Hazel," Auphel said as I leaned my face against a cool stone wall and caught my breath. "I expected they'd have cleaned up."

I waited until the spots cleared before I tried to walk away. "This is what they were doing last night?" I was glad that Auphel had been with me, but felt sick thinking she'd known about this.

She picked at her rough fingernails and bit her lip. "I suppose. I mean, I didn't know exactly, but I knew they were still hunting down a few important people. Personal enemies. Slavers." She glanced up at a nearby storefront. "A garment maker who..." She looked back. "Hazel, he kept imps tied to his machines and cut their feet off if they tried to escape."

"That was a woman's leg."

"Maybe it was his wife."

"And what did she do?"

Auphel looked away. "Nothing."

"I see." And I did. These humans had invited their fates with their actions or lack thereof. I couldn't say they didn't deserve to die. Even if I'd never suffered as these monsters had, I understood why "an eye for an eye" would be so appealing.

And yet an old quote about that leaving the whole world blind wouldn't leave my mind.

I clutched the skeleton key tighter and walked faster. I didn't want to see. Didn't want to have to think about it.

This has nothing to do with me. I'm going to find a way home. Soon.

We continued on and entered the square where the angel had been executed—if, in fact, he'd been alive to begin with. I wanted to ask about that. Zinian said Verelle had created them. Did they think or feel? Or were they empty shells?

I would have asked Auphel if my train of thought hadn't crashed and derailed at the sight of the pile of books in the middle of the square, a mountain of paper and leather that rose higher than Auphel's head. She urged me on, but I couldn't stop watching—not only out of curiosity over the books, but out of fascination with the three giants who were dumping more onto the top of the pile as fast as the books slid down. The creatures stood at least twenty feet tall, clothed in rags that could have at one time been boat sails. The closest had one massive eye in the centre of his deeply lined forehead. The other beside him had two, in the same glacier blue shade. Their hair matched as well, fiery red from head to hairy toes. Behind them, a massive woman who sported impressively thick black hair turned toward me as she dropped more books onto the pile. She had three eyes, the third set in her forehead just above and between the other two.

The ground shook under their footsteps.

"What are they doing?" I asked Auphel.

She looked around. "Clearing out the library. I'm guessing we're to have another bonfire tonight."

"To celebrate again?"

"General Grys has permitted the destruction of the human things." Auphel moved toward the pile, gave a friendly wave to one of the giants, and picked up a book. I did the same, selecting a beautiful volume with a gilded blue cover. The pages inside had been hand-printed and gorgeously illuminated. I'd practiced my own handwriting plenty over the past few years— another calming exercise, one that filled dozens of notebooks and planners. These books put my work to shame.

"They can't destroy these," I said.

Auphel sighed. "I know. We'd do so much better to save some for winter, when we'll actually need them."

"I mean that they're irreplaceable. Once these burn, they're gone. An entire culture. Right?" From the way Grys and his council had spoken of the villages, it sounded like there probably weren't a lot of other libraries holding similar collections.

"Not all cultures deserve to be saved," Auphel said.

"But what about their knowledge?" I climbed up the pile to reach a book that lay open to a picture of a tree. Each page held a similar image of a plant, all labelled and marked with medicinal or culinary uses. "What about the things they've learned that would be good for everyone else to know?"

Auphel's brow furrowed. "We're fine on our own." But she sounded doubtful.

"What about magic?" I asked more quietly, and my chest tightened at the realization of what might be about to go up in flames. "What if my answer is in there, and they burn it?"

Auphel didn't answer.

"Are you sure this is what Grys wanted?" I searched the faces around the square, as though someone in authority might suddenly appear. "Is he even in charge?"

Auphel tossed her book onto the pile as another load skittered down, dumped from above by the giants. "He's the leader we have. He's not a king or a mayor. We don't have that yet. Right now we're to be free, to do as we see fit, and to get rid of the human things. That *is* an order."

"This is a mistake," I said, more to myself than Auphel. Even though I didn't adore all books, even though I knew Auphel might be right that these weren't all valuable, I felt a deep and instinctive revulsion at the thought of them being destroyed without question. And maybe the books weren't mine to save, but there was a good chance that the information in them could be my only hope of ever getting home.

"Even if you're right, no one will listen if you try to stop them." Auphel nodded toward the giants, then at a small group of gaublings that stood in the shadows of a nearby building who watched us with sharp and mistrustful eyes. "Maybe where you come from, these things are important. Maybe people listen to you there. Here, you're a human. If you try to save these books, it's only going to get them burned faster. And maybe you with them."

I clutched the botany book to my chest and backed away. The gaublings stepped closer. I couldn't help but notice their sharp teeth as they raised their lips to snarl at me.

"Hazel, put it down," Auphel said. "Let's just go to the palace and rest. You can look at the books there. You can't stop this."

Something Zinian had said the day before came back to me.

"I know I can't," I said. "But I might know someone who can."

I turned and ran.

7

A uphel's heavy footsteps ran close behind me, the uneven silences between filled with the pitter patter of the gaublings' smaller, quicker feet. One of them shrieked right behind me. I glanced over my shoulder to see Auphel grab a gaubling by the scruff of his neck. She held him until we passed a soft-looking pile of discarded human clothes outside of a cottage, then tossed him into it.

She reached for me. I darted around the corner, and she missed. The palace came into sight, all white spires and shining gold, and I ran harder. A stitch formed in my side. I hadn't been a runner since I'd quit track and field in sixth grade. Still, I kept ahead of the lumbering ogress and the short-legged gaublings, racing to find Zinian.

The wrong turns we'd made earlier fouled me up, but I found the corridor to the meeting room. The door opened as I approached, and Jaid stepped out.

I slid to a halt before I ran into her. She closed the door tight.

"What's all this racket?"

"I need to speak with Zinian," I gasped, pressing a hand to my side. "Please."

"He's busy. As are we all." One feline ear twitched, and her tail cut sharp arcs through the air behind her. She glared upward as Auphel approached, breathing hard and limping worse than she had before. "You were supposed to keep an eye on her."

"Sorry, Lieutenant." Auphel looked at me, appearing more hurt than angry. "I don't know what got into her."

"I have information that Zinian will be interested in," I said.

She folded her arms across her chest. "Tell me. I'll pass it along."

Something told me that no matter how I phrased it, Jaid would see no point in preserving the books. And maybe she would be right. This was stupid. I had no connection to the people of this city, no reason to care if their knowledge burned. Except that I did. Libraries and bookstores were safe places. Rich places. Dusty and quiet and predictable places. At least, they always had been for me. Havens full of knowledge.

It wasn't my city. It wasn't my library. I didn't care. I couldn't watch it burn, and I couldn't let what might be my only chance of ending this nightmare go up with it.

This is too risky, objected the part of my brain that usually controlled my emotions and my actions. *Back down now.*

Not this time.

I clutched the book to my chest and straightened my shoulders. "I need to speak to him myself."

"No. In fact—"

The door opened behind her, and Zinian stepped out.

"What's going on out here?" He frowned at me. "You shouldn't be here."

"Please," I said. "They're going to burn all of the books from the library."

"As they've been ordered to do," Zinian said quietly. "This is not a situation you want to involve yourself in, Hazel."

"But so much could be lost." I glanced at Jaid and wished she'd leave. Her eyes seemed to cut me every time she shot me one of her disgusted looks.

Zinian took the book from me and flipped through it slowly, as though absorbing the images. "Better to make a clean start."

I took a deep breath to steady my nerves. "With respect, there's no such thing."

He raised an eyebrow. "No?"

Think, Hazel. This was basic negotiation. I couldn't ask them to save the library because I wanted to see whether it held my answers, or because I wanted to keep a familiar place where I would feel safe while I learned how to escape from this strange world. No, I had to think of what *they* would get out of saving it.

I forced myself to ignore Jaid's glare and Auphel's hurt expression, and focused on Zinian. When I looked into his eyes, it was almost possible to forget how monstrous he was. *They're reasonable people,* I reminded myself, protecting themselves from the real monsters.

"What if the answer to Verelle's disappearance is in those books?" I asked. "What if they're about to burn your only chance at finding and finishing her?"

Jaid hissed. "She has no idea what she's talking about, Zin. Verelle is gone, and Grys has called off the hunt. For your own sake, forget this. You said you would."

Zinian gave her a sharp look. "I'm well aware of what I've agreed to." When he turned to me, his eyes remained hard, but there was no anger there. I'd never been good at reading people, but I thought I read interest in his keen gaze. "You may be correct, Hazel. And I imagine you've considered the fact that the books may contain answers regarding your own journey home. But I can't walk into that room and say we have to restore the library for the sake of one human or my own lingering..." He paused, searching for the right word.

"Obsession," Jaid offered. "Think of your reputation. If you stand before Grys and show any weakness toward a human or their culture, it will confirm everything your detractors say about you. If anything, you should stand in the square tonight and drop the torch that starts the fire. Seal your position. Claim the victory, remind them who made it possible. You've been too quiet since Verelle disappeared. Too absent from the streets."

The relief I felt at hearing he hadn't been out there ripping off people's legs hit me hard. *It doesn't mean he's safe,* I reminded myself.

Zinian rolled his shoulders back and flexed his wings. "You see the problem, Hazel?"

I didn't think I saw all of it, but it gave me an idea of what he was up against. He'd mentioned how his human aspects had set him apart from other monsters, but I suspected it went deeper than that. Zinian's position seemed to be nearly as precarious as mine.

"You can't ask the general to save the library for my sake, or for yours."

Jaid flicked an ear. "She can be taught. Incredible." She leaned against the wall and tapped her claws against the dark stone. The casual pose did nothing to make her seem less dangerous. "Go back to Verelle's rooms, human Hazel." She glared at Auphel. "And stay out of the way, this time."

I ignored the claws, my trembling heart, and the sweat that had formed on my forehead in spite of the cool air. Zinian was still listening, so I focused on him again.

"There's a saying in my world that those who forget the past are doomed to repeat it," I said. Jaid narrowed her eyes, but didn't interrupt me. "The history of your world seems as cold and cruel as mine, but surely forgetting isn't the answer. At least make sure you're not throwing the baby out with the bathwater."

Zinian's brow furrowed. "Excuse me?"

"I mean..." I shrugged. It seemed my ability to speak and understand their language didn't extend to idioms. "Maybe a lot of what's there in those books is bad. But maybe there's some knowledge that should be salvaged. And maybe it's better not to forget where the humans went so wrong. If we—if you, I mean, could learn how they thought, what they believed, how they became the horrible creatures they were, it would benefit your new society so much."

"We won't repeat their mistakes," Jaid growled. "We're nothing like you."

I forced myself to look at her without flinching. "Then let it be a monument to their foolishness. Build your new city in the remains of the old, and let the library stand as a reminder of what you overcame."

"She has nothing to do with any of this," Jaid reminded Zinian.

"I know," Zinian said, but one corner of his mouth had turned up slightly as I spoke. His reaction pleased me, and I told myself it was only because it gave me hope for the library. "But that doesn't mean she's wrong. What if Verelle found a way back? What if another enemy rose some day? We'd be better prepared to fight if we had this knowledge."

Jaid's ears lay flat against the smooth curves of her skull. "This is insanity."

"No. It might be the first sane idea we've heard in days, since the destruction and killing began. I'll speak to Grys."

Jaid's lip lifted in a snarl. "Fine. But be sure to discuss the punishment for a human's insubordination when meddling in the affairs of monsters. We need to set a proper precedent."

Zinian nodded without looking at me and returned to the meeting room with Jaid close behind.

"What does that mean?" I asked Auphel. "Punishment?"

She didn't answer.

"Auphel, I'm sorry. I didn't think about this getting you in trouble. I shouldn't have run, but you see why this is important, don't you?"

She let out a heavy sigh. "I don't know. I'd just as soon see the books gone, myself, but Zinian seems to understand." She twirled the hem of her shirt around her fingers. "I thought we were going to be friends, you and me."

"I want that, too. Would it help if I promised not to run from you again?"

She nodded, but I supposed I had a lot of work to do if I wanted to regain her trust. I hoped Zinian would be persuasive, that I hadn't just hurt Auphel and pissed Jaid off for nothing.

We walked back to Verelle's rooms.

"Auphel, what did Jaid mean about punishment?"

She shrugged. "When humans kept us as servants and slaves, we weren't allowed to talk back or have ideas unless they asked us something—and then our ideas became their ideas. If you didn't follow the rules, you were beaten. Or killed, if you weren't useful enough. Guess things are flipped upside down now."

"I'm not a servant or a slave," I said quietly.

"You're a human, and it's not your world. Why do you think I tried so hard to stop you when you ran?"

My stomach clenched. Speaking up and risking confrontation had been terrifying, but it had seemed worthwhile. I remembered the massive axe that Auphel had wielded the night we met, and a chill came over me.

This is why I never stick my neck out, I thought. *You never know when it's going to end with losing your head.*

8

Auphel came out of the pantry covered in flour. She sneezed, sending a cloud of white dust into the air. "Is this enough?"

"Should be. Enough to give it a try, anyway."

She'd agreed to take me to the palace kitchens that afternoon to find my own meal. In spite of my current anxiety over my future, my stomach kept insisting it needed to be fed. The squashed tomatoes Auphel brought me weren't keeping me full, and I suspected I should keep my strength up.

The kitchens were better stocked than I'd expected. No refrigerator, but there was a deep pantry with a cold storage room containing pickled vegetables in clay pots. I couldn't find any meat, but there was butter and a few eggs. Any food that might have been prepared before the attack on the palace was long gone, but I could work with this.

I hoped.

Auphel, who had no experience with cooking, seemed surprised that I might be willing to eat such things. She helped me build a fire in the stone oven that covered a wall of the kitchen. I had no idea how to control the temperature, but we had the place to ourselves. Trial and error would have to work out eventually.

The kitchen became hot enough that my dress stuck to my sweaty body. I tied my hair up, but the shorter locks at the front kept falling down as I kneaded my attempt at bread. I brushed the strands aside with dough-covered hands, and they stuck in place.

We left the kitchen to visit the orchard, and Auphel gleefully hacked apart far more apples than I needed. I mixed them with butter and something that smelled like cinnamon, then wrapped the mess inside a flat slab of dough.

"That looks horrid," Auphel noted, though not without great interest. "Humans have such strange tastes."

"It will probably taste horrid, too. I've never been much of a cook. More of a takeout girl."

Auphel's confused look led to a discussion about my world that carried us through the time it took the makeshift apple flip to bake… or rather, through the time it took to burn on the outside while remaining raw in the middle, and then through the process of trying again.

Explaining the use of telephones and computers to order food was nearly impossible.

"So it's like I said. You do know magic."

"No, we really don't have it in my world. It's technology. Research and experimentation and… physics." I shrugged helplessly. "I don't know how it all works, exactly."

"But you can talk to another human on the other side of the world. Even see them."

"Right."

"Because of the electri-thingy. And machines with tiny parts that remember things without them being written down. They're just… there."

I laughed. "There are people in my world who could explain it. I'm just not one of them."

She gave me a look that said I must be pulling her leg about the whole thing.

We sat together on the floor, and I offered her a bite of the pastry (which was still a bit doughy in the middle, but quite delicious). She pronounced it "not bad," but refused seconds. "Ogres don't go in for baked goods and such," she said. "Some of the palace monsters were cooks for the humans, but I don't think you'll have much luck getting them to help you."

"No. It's a start, though." I could work with this bread, and I'd see what else I could salvage in the garden. Surely there had to be meat around somewhere, but I didn't want to ask. They'd probably tell me I'd have to kill it myself.

The door swung open. Zinian stepped in, looking serious, and I held back the urge to vomit my meal all over the smooth stone floor at the realization that my punishment had come. Maybe I shouldn't be worrying about food if I was doomed anyway.

He nodded cordially to Auphel. "Having fun?" he asked.

"I was. Why are you… What's happening?" Her brow furrowed.

"I need to speak with Hazel alone."

My heart stilled. *It will be fine. Nothing to worry about. It's just a terrifying monster who hates humans coming to tell you how you'll be punished for pissing them all off. Not a big deal.*

I forced myself to stand. He'd already seen me on my knees, begging for my life. I didn't feel like repeating that. I doubted I had it in me to go out with grace and dignity, but he might listen to a rational argument.

At least they hadn't sent Jaid or that other ogre. Zinian was reasonable, if not necessarily soft-hearted.

I tried not to remember the cold hate in his eyes when he'd snapped the head off the human doll.

Auphel shuffled away as Zinian stepped closer to me. "You won't just take her away without telling me, will you?" she asked, her voice timid.

Zinian smiled at her, with more warmth than I'd seen in him before. "You'll know before anything happens, I promise."

I supposed that should make me feel better. It didn't.

After Auphel left, Zinian looked around the kitchen. "Quite the mess."

"I know. I'll clean it up. If I get a chance, I mean."

"Hmm. Shall we talk outside?"

As we walked, I noted that the pants he now wore were clean and far less ragged than the others had been. Still no shirt. I supposed it might be hard to find one that fit his shape—the broad shoulders, the extra muscles on his chest and back, and the wings that needed so much room to move. All told, it wasn't a bad view—or it wouldn't have been if my mind had been in any kind of shape to appreciate such things.

Or if we weren't different species.

More importantly, I noted that he wasn't carrying any weapons. Though he couldn't leave his claws, horns, or teeth behind, he'd done me the courtesy of removing his sword.

"Do I at least get a trial?" I asked as we stepped into the cooler air of the kitchen garden.

Zinian didn't answer until we'd passed through the smashed door into the orchard. "No."

"I see."

He turned to face me and crossed his arms. "Grys agreed to preserve the library. Books from houses and shops will be burned tonight, along with other items we wish to see destroyed. But he agrees that we could benefit from keeping the memory of what we survived, and that there may turn out to be information there we won't want to lose yet."

I relaxed slightly. At least it wasn't all for nothing.

"I had to tell him it was mostly my idea," he continued. "If he knew the arguments came from you, it would have been the end of the discussion."

"Fine by me." The less Grys thought about me, the better. "Does that mean I'm not in trouble?"

"No. I told him that you'd brought the issue to my attention."

"Why—Oh. You don't want Jaid to be angry with you."

It hadn't been a question, but he nodded. "She's not wrong about my situation. If anyone so much as suspects that I'm protecting you, it will cause trouble for me. Jaid is an old friend, and the last person I can afford to offend. So while we may in the end be grateful for your intervention, Grys ordered me to think of an appropriate way to remind you of your proper place in this world."

He flexed his fingers and looked down at his dark claws.

A chill came over me, and I felt ill again. "What is it?"

"It's terrible."

"Tell me!"

He took a deep breath. "You're to be sentenced to reorganization of the library."

"What?" My stomach dropped. "That's it? I expected you to say you had to break my legs, or whip me, or…" I felt light-headed, and sat on the ground next to a broken tomato plant. I rubbed a leaf between my fingers, releasing their comfortingly familiar, earthy scent.

He smiled down at me.

"So you do have a sense of humour," I said when I was able to raise my head from between my knees. "I was beginning to wonder."

"There hasn't been much call for one for some time," he said, and offered a hand to pull me to my feet. His smile had disappeared, but his grasp was gentle. "The punishment is no joke. You may soon wish you had been whipped. At least that would be done quickly. We'll have the giants move the books back to the building for you before dark, but you will be responsible for the rest of it. Sort through, see what's worth salvaging and what's not, re-shelve them. I imagine the shelves will need to be rebuilt in places, and the clean-up required will be significant. There's a human apartment on the top level of the building, and you'll live there."

He tilted his head to one side. "Under Auphel's care, of course. It's going to take ages to get all of that done. And I suppose by the time you've finished all of that, you'll be asked to stay on. You'll be the only one with any idea where to find things. Might be hard for you to leave and go to a human settlement in the country. You'll be trapped here with your key and all these doors it will surely never unlock, though I have no doubt you'll keep trying." Zinian set his fists on his hips and seemed to have a hard time holding back a grin. "It's the cruelest punishment I could think of."

I smiled, slowly. "Terrible. You should watch yourself from here on out. I know how to hold a grudge."

In fact, I didn't. I'd never liked grudges any more than I'd liked confrontations or unpredictable situations.

"Thank you," I said. Something passed between us then. Mutual understanding, at the very least. I decided that I wanted to know more about him. He was intriguing, not to mention tolerant of me. I needed as many friends as I could get here, even if those friends had made streets run red with blood.

His humour made him seem more familiar and friendly, revealing a side of him I thought I could like quite a lot. Maybe nothing in this world was black and white, any more than it was in mine.

I caught my gaze slipping down the hard planes of his upper body and forced myself to look at his eyes.

Friends, Hazel. You need friends. That's all.

He cleared his throat. "You're welcome. I don't imagine this will be an easy adjustment for you, being here. But at least you'll have something to do, and I'll see that you're compensated for your work." He frowned. "But don't expect this sort of lenience again. If you get it into your head to step out of line and it reflects badly on me—"

"I won't. I'll be good as… as…" Not gold. They didn't pay for anything with it. "I'll be good," I finished.

"I hope so. You have a promising mind, and I believe a far kinder spirit than the humans of this world. If you can find a way to fit in here, I think you could do quite well. Give it time, though."

The way he looked at me made me uncomfortable. As though he was studying me and liked what he saw.

"I should go," I said, at the same time as he said, "Have supper with me tonight."

"What?"

He smiled, awkwardly this time. "You look like you could use a good meal. I'm curious to hear about where you come from, and thought you might wish to learn a little more about our world." He shrugged one shoulder. "I have no desire to attend the bonfire, and everyone else will be gone."

The idea of being alone with him in the palace made me shiver, and yet I wasn't afraid he'd hurt me. Not now. His eyes looked deep into mine, searching for something. They were quite beautiful, really. Like liquid emeralds.

I straightened my shoulders. "That sounds quite pleasant. Thank you."

I'm not attracted to him, I decided. I was objectively aware of his attractiveness as a creature. That was all. I ignored the warmth that shot through me when he smiled again, a slightly roguish glint in his eyes.

A monster and a human couldn't... I mean, surely even in this world it wouldn't be... Would it?

Hazel. No.

The very idea of searching for love back home had frayed my nerves since I'd booted jackass of the year out of my heart, and the risks would be far greater here, even with a human.

Which he's definitely not.

I followed him into the kitchen where Auphel waited. "What's happening?" she asked.

"It's fine," I told her. "We're moving out of the palace. I'll explain later."

Her massive shoulders relaxed. "That's good news."

Zinian reached the door and turned back.

"Hazel?"

"Yes?"

He gave me a quick once-over and pressed his lips together. "You might want to see about a bath before supper."

It wasn't until he left and I found a shiny pot I could use as a mirror that I realized he'd been trying to bite back a laugh. My hair was streaked with hardened bread dough, and a smudge of flour covered the bridge of my nose.

And I'd looked this fantastic the whole time we'd been speaking. Whatever I'd thought might have passed between us had nothing to do with my own appeal, that was for certain.

"At least I know he's not interested in any funny business," I muttered, and scrubbed my nose with the filthy sleeve of my dress. The realization brought as much relief as embarrassment.

I loosened the ribbon that held my hair, but the grease and dough kept it solidly in place. I was suddenly aware of how dirty my feet were—I'd abandoned the golden slippers after they got blood on them, and had found nothing to replace them. *I must smell lovely.*

"Auphel, are there baths here?"

She grinned. "I thought you'd never ask."

9

After unheated baths in massive white marble tubs in a room with an incredible view of the sprawling city below, Auphel and I hurried back to Verelle's rooms. I didn't think of them as my rooms, and was glad that I never would. Though the space was beautiful, rich, and relaxing, I wanted nothing to do with this mysterious queen. I was stuck with her wardrobe, but at least that would be the extent of it as soon as I moved to the library.

Auphel lounged on the carpet, picking at loose fibres, as I laid dresses out on the bed.

"The white one is nice," she offered.

I held the gauzy fabric against myself in front of the mirror. "It's gorgeous, but it won't work. The open neckline would be too showy for someone with my curves."

She nodded. "Verelle looked like you could snap her in half as easy as a twig. You seem more solid."

"Thanks, Auphel." That might not have been a compliment where I came from, but she obviously meant it to be. I had to keep reminding myself that this was a different world. I couldn't expect anyone here to understand why showing off that much skin would bother me.

But why shouldn't I wear something eye-catching? I was the only human around, and it wasn't as though Zinian was going to care any more than I would if a dog wore a sweater that didn't fit right.

Still, I couldn't help wondering about that as I slipped into the white gown and turned in front of the mirror. The dress was far more revealing than anything I'd have dared at home. The top was well-constructed enough, but gave the appearance of being little more than two broad strips of fabric, gathered at the shoulders and crossed at the front to attach to the waistline of the flowing, many-layered skirt. I imagined Zinian's bright green eyes looking me over, and my heart skipped.

Stop being a friggin' idiot.

I turned to Auphel. "Does this look silly?"

She shrugged. "I don't understand human fashions. But you look nice. You should leave your hair down. Humans here always wore it up."

"Hmm." Without a blow-dryer or straightener, my hair was quickly drying into a mess of loose waves, looking a little flat at the top. I compromised by choosing a blue and silver comb from Verelle's dressing table that I used to hold my hair back on one side. *Better. But...*

I leaned closer to the mirror and frowned. It had been years since I'd wanted to leave the house without foundation and mascara as a bare minimum. Though my acne wasn't quite as bad as it had been a few years before, my skin was dotted with the shadows of scars across my chin and forehead, and I broke out once a month like hormone-driven clockwork. My mother had taught me to cover them up when I was fourteen, and I'd never looked back.

I dug through the drawers and was pleased to find a few promising items housed in beautiful cut-glass jars—red cream for lips and cheeks, dark inky liquid for lining eyes, browns and blues for eyelids. I rubbed a little of a pale apricot-coloured cream on the back of one hand and drew a sharp breath as it made my veins invisible and the wrinkles on my knuckles disappear. It blended perfectly to my slightly paler skin tone and tingled pleasantly as my skin drank it in.

"I could make a fortune with this stuff at home," I mused, and spread a little along my jawline to test the colour there.

Auphel hauled herself up from the floor and sat on the edge of the bed to watch. She wrinkled her nose. "What are you doing?"

"Making myself pretty."

She sighed. "Verelle's secret weapon, I suppose."

I paused and watched the cream smooth my skin. "Monsters don't use this, do you?"

"Not at all. I don't understand it. Why would you want to cover your beautiful face markings?"

I watched her in the mirror, watching me. I'd considered her ugly when we first met, but now I thought nothing of her strange appearance. She was Auphel. Not an ogress or a terrifying monster, but my kind-hearted friend. And as our eyes met in the mirror, I understood that she was beautiful. Not as my world judged beauty, but on her own terms. The dark blotches on her green skin reminded me of lichen on rocks hidden in a mysterious forest. Her black eyes held the depths of the night sky, and her massive, protruding jaw displayed her incredible strength. The graceless limp she walked with and the scars on her arms showed that she'd lived a hard life and come through it stronger and wiser.

And here I was worried that a few blemishes would turn the stomach of a horned demon monster. I shook my head at myself.

I didn't know how I was supposed to make myself presentable when human beauty was an abomination, but I knew I wanted to distance myself from the humans of this world.

I grabbed a cloth and rubbed the makeup off my face, trying to ignore the blossoming realization that I was going to be very lonely indeed if I couldn't go home. Jake had been a shit boyfriend, and no great loss, but I would miss that kind of relationship. I knew I could make it alone, but I wanted someone to laugh with, to cuddle with at night, to love passionately.

And a life of celibacy... how horrible.

I pushed those thoughts aside. Things had changed, and I was the only human in town. Nothing to be done about it until I found a way to use the key again.

"Better?" I asked as I turned around, bare-faced.

Auphel's eyes disappeared in deep wrinkles as she smiled. "Much."

I ran my fingers through my hair again. "You must think I'm so silly. Do you mind doing all this? Finding me food and following me around? I promise I'll be more self-sufficient soon."

She leaned back on the bed. "No. I didn't like you running from me, but I'm glad they think you need guarding. This is much nicer than fighting, or whatever they'd have me do next."

I sat next to her and tucked my legs under my skirt.

"The war must have been horrible for you."

She nodded. "I was barely beginning my adult years when they took me for the army. I didn't know anything outside of my home and my family. I'd tussled with my brothers, of course. They hurt me, I hurt them... I miss them sometimes. But that didn't prepare me for real fighting. Killing." She rubbed her leg, then lay silent for a moment, staring at the ceiling. "I have terrible dreams about the people I killed and about friends I lost in the battles. I'm happy to be here with you instead of in the streets."

She drew in a deep, shuddering breath, then sat up and smiled. "We should go."

My heart ached for her. She had the body of a fighter, but had been cursed with the heart of a lamb. It was a wonder it hadn't all broken her completely. I didn't think I could have survived it.

She led me down the halls and up a flight of stairs. "Will you attend the fire tonight?" I asked. "Since you're not on duty."

"I might just rest. Wander a bit."

She stopped in front of a wooden door and raised her fist to knock. The door swung open, and Zinian ducked out of the way before she could punch him in the face. He wore a shirt this time, a fitted tunic that had been tailored to leave his wings free.

He leaned out into the hallway and glanced both ways, as though checking to see whether anyone might be watching. "Thank you, Auphel. I'll return her safely later tonight."

Auphel pressed a hand to her chest, open-palmed, spun on her heel, and walked away. A salute, I supposed.

Zinian motioned for me to enter, and I stepped into his room.

The walls were lined with books, and the bed was covered in heavy red blankets. A table for two had been set with cutlery and long-stemmed water glasses in the open space near the roaring fire, which was safely contained by a metal grate in the heavy granite fireplace. The carpet was thicker and softer than the one in Verelle's room, and I curled my bare toes into it.

"It's not bad, is it?" Zinian asked. I turned and found him smiling slightly as he watched me. "This was the queen's chief advisor's room."

"It's lovely," I said. I looked over the books again, and a tingle of embarrassment crept over the back of my neck. "I guess maybe the main library wasn't so essential, after all. I never considered how many books they probably had here in the palace. Why didn't you say something?"

He stepped closer. "Because preserving those books may help protect these ones, and I do have a certain affection for books, as a rule. Because we haven't done any sort of inventory of what's here or there, and you're right. There may be something useful." His gaze dropped lower, taking in my dress and everything it revealed, and heat crept into my cheeks as he drew in a long, slow breath. He met my eyes again. "Because you seemed so passionate about it, and I thought you might need that library as much as anyone. You don't seem the type to enjoy being locked up with nothing to do. And you should be happy, if you have to stay."

"Thank you." My voice came out softer than I'd intended. "I have been feeling lost. It will be better when I have some kind of purpose."

He motioned for me to sit, then carried over two covered plates from another table in the corner. I felt faint at the scent that wafted from mine as he uncovered it, rich and thick and promising more flavour than I'd enjoyed in days. Vegetables again, but smothered in a butter and herb sauce, and accompanied by some unfamiliar grain dish.

My stomach groaned.

Zinian's meal was the same, save for the addition of a slab of meat, seared on the outside. He saw me looking and raised an eyebrow. "Does this bother you?"

"What is it?"

"Cow. I can put it away if it's a problem."

"Why would that bother me? It looks lovely."

He stared at me for a few seconds, then laughed. "I'm sorry. I keep forgetting you're not necessarily like the humans here. You eat meat?"

"Are you kidding?"

"Would you like some?" He picked up a sharp knife and cut the meat open. The inside was cooked, but barely. Bright red blood stained the rest of the food on his plate.

"Um…Sure." I enjoyed rare beef. This was just a little more of the same.

We ate in silence. I couldn't have talked if I'd needed to—I was too busy shovelling the divine food into my mouth. Fresh peas exploded with bright flavour on my tongue. I'd never cared for them before, but found myself suddenly in love. It was gone all too soon.

"Who made this," I asked, "and where have they been hiding the past few days?"

"I did. We've started bringing food in from the farms outside the city."

"Wha—I mean, wow. Thank you."

He nodded and sipped his water. "Tell me more about your world. I suppose it must be quite different. Meat-eating humans are a good start."

I told him a few things I thought he might find interesting, given what I knew about their world. It made me realize how shallow my knowledge of things like economics and politics were. He asked a little about my life, my schooling, and the town where I grew up. And he listened. Not the way most people listen, as though they're organizing their thoughts and waiting for their next chance to speak, but actually *listening*. His eyes never left mine, save to glance at the door when the faint sounds of footsteps went by. The monstrous aspects of his appearance seemed to fade away. Not that they disappeared—I was still aware of the horns, the wings, the claws. They just didn't matter.

"So this fellow you lived with," he said. "Will he be worried that you're missing?"

"I doubt he'll notice. I made it very clear that I didn't want to speak to him again."

"Is that common in your culture? These intense relationships ending?"

My cheeks warmed. "It is when one of the partners goes on business trips and sleeps with every waitress who catches his eye on the road."

"Ah." He offered a sympathetic grimace. "I suppose I won't offer my regrets if you're better off without him."

"Thank you."

Silence followed, and I wasn't entirely sure whether it was awkward or not. I broke it by saying, "I guess I'll have to get used to the differences, if I'm staying here."

"Elurien is different," he agreed. "Even from itself a few months ago. Things have been bad for everyone, but in spite of what you've seen since you arrived, we are trying to create a better future."

I rolled the stem of my water glass between my fingers. "And what about your future, personally? Now that the fighting seems to be done and Verelle is gone?"

He frowned at her name. "I don't know. I won't stay here, which should please many." He said it without self-pity, but it made me curious.

"You seem to have a strange relationship with the others," I said cautiously, well aware that he might care more about that than he let on. "You're one of their leaders, right?"

"I am. And they take orders from me well enough. But it took me a long time to gain even that much respect, and now that they don't need me, it's better that I go. I look too human to be trusted."

"I'm surprised they're so shallow," I said. "You look perfectly monstrous to me."

He flashed me half a smile. "I appreciate that. But the fact is that I must have quite a bit of human blood in me somewhere. You've never met an amalgus?"

"Can't say I have."

"Amalgi aren't a proper species. We're a little of our amalgus parent and a little of the other one, and it all comes out like… well." He gestured to his own body. "Like so. I don't know anything about either of my parents. I was abandoned at birth and taken in by a harpy."

"That's terrible."

He shrugged. "It's how it goes. Inter-species relationships are generally frowned upon, which leaves my kind alone much of the time, as we're quite rare. Giving birth to a child like me would have been shameful for anyone. The fact that I lived at all was probably a mercy on my mother's part, especially if she was human."

"I see." So it hadn't been cockiness when he implied that he got stared at a lot. He was unusual, even here. A misjudgment on my part, if a small one.

I tried to imagine what would have compelled a human woman of this world to make a mistake like that. But then, if Zinian's father had been anything like him, I couldn't blame her. His appearance had been shocking at first, but once I'd got past my fear and noticed his intelligence and compassion, he'd become rather distracting. I suddenly became aware again of my exposed skin, the alluring dress I'd worn. Had I really thought he wouldn't care? That he couldn't want me? He'd said it was frowned-upon, not impossible.

Focus, girl. As far as I was concerned, any physical attraction I felt could sit its ass down and shut up. His words were far more important, and I suspected he needed a listening ear more than anything else I had to offer.

I didn't ask more, but waited until he was ready to speak again.

He frowned. "It goes deeper, though. I'm not their leader because of a brilliant military career. They needed me because I knew the palace well, and knew Verelle better than anyone. She hid behind her magic and her walls for hundreds of years, but she had a few weaknesses. One of them was that she grew bored with human company after a dozen or so decades." He hesitated over the word *company*. "She chose monsters as her personal attendants. Always those with more pleasing human-like faces or bodies. We all knew about it, and our parents tried to protect those of us who might be vulnerable."

"How bad was it to be chosen?"

"It was a death sentence. Verelle couldn't afford to have her secrets get out. When she grew bored of her servants and playthings, she had them beheaded. Whether it was the young centaur who drew her bathwater or the masked gorgon she kept as a symbol of her power and control, no one lasted more than a few years in the palace. And depending on what games struck her fancy at any time, death might have been a mercy."

He dragged his claws lightly over the scars on his right cheek. "She spotted me when she passed through a forest where I was hunting, and liked what she saw. When they came for me, I tried to tear my face off. I hoped that she might leave me alone if she found me hideous." He smiled sadly. "She had me beaten for defacing her property, but forgave it soon enough. Gave me a place as her personal scribe. Among other things."

I wasn't sure what to say, except...

"I'm sorry." I thought I understood what his other duties might have involved, and wouldn't pry more into that. I felt my cheeks flush slightly as I considered my own response to him as I'd got past the whole monster thing. *I'm not like her, I swear.*

He stood and walked to the bookshelf beside the fireplace, where he ran his fingertips gently over the spines of the books. "I got used to life here, and as I got to know Verelle better, I thought perhaps I could change her mind about monsters by making her see me as more than a rebellious beast."

He clenched his hands into fists. "So I stopped fighting her. I obeyed willingly. And for a long time, it appeared to be working. She seemed genuinely fond of me, and she let her guard down. Gave me a little freedom. Even if I couldn't return her affection, I tolerated it." His brow furrowed. "I gave up my pride and dignity in an attempt at peace.

"She never grew tired of me, never took a second companion while I served her. And her personal servants were treated well while I was there. I heard less talk of war. I was keeping everyone safe by making her happy, or so I thought."

"And she chose not to kill you, obviously."

He turned back to me. His skin had lost some of its colour. "She would have, eventually, yet I stayed for the sake of the others. Then one day I found her in the dungeons. A male centaur stood chained to the wall as a human woman whipped him and cut him with knives. A female centaur lay in the corner, already broken and half dead, sobbing. The floor was red with their blood. I learned later that they were lovers, torn apart to work in separate mines and reunited in that dungeon after years apart. Verelle had promised them they would leave alive and together if they watched each other's torture without attacking the humans who kept their mate chained, and without screaming."

"My God." My stomach filled with ice as I listened, and gooseflesh covered me.

"Verelle wore a white dress, splattered with blood."

I glanced down at the dress I'd borrowed from her closet and wished I had chosen another colour. Zinian didn't seem to notice. "She'd stood that close to watch. Her eyes were so bright, her cheeks flushed, like when…" He bared his fangs. "It was all a lie. I was never enough, and was never really changing her darker attitudes toward monsters. She just hid some of her pleasures from me. Keeping me complacent was as much of a game for her as torturing the centaurs was. I escaped not long after that, tracked down the rebellion, and told Grys that I could get his soldiers into the city and the palace. It took years, but we built the perfect army to fight Verelle. I taught them to recognize her illusions and exploit the weaknesses in the winged soldiers she'd created. I'd kept my eyes and ears open while I lived in the palace, and it paid off. But no one has ever forgotten how I gained that knowledge."

"You had no choice."

He shook his head. "I could have fought, as the others did. I suppose she would have enjoyed that, but at least I could have tried. In the end I only angered her. Things didn't end well for any of her slaves or servants after I left, and the humans' mistreatment of us only became worse." He swallowed hard and looked around the room. His wings flexed. "I took a chance, and I suppose in the end it worked out, but I still don't know whether the cost to myself or anyone else was worth it. So no, I won't be staying in this city. And I don't blame the others for hating me."

Again, I didn't know what to say. As far as I could see, he'd had the best intentions when he'd complied with whatever Verelle had asked of him. He'd tried to save his people by serving their enemy, and for that the others saw him as a traitor. His regrets ran deeper than anything I'd ever experienced, and my heart ached for him.

"It must be hard, but at least you made a choice," I said before I'd realized I was speaking aloud. He looked at me, and I made myself go on. "I've never had to take that kind of a chance. I thought that leaving home was a risk, moving in with someone, falling in love. They were small things, though. Your choices hurt more people than mine have, but I think they were also less selfish than any risk I've ever taken. I've always been too scared. I admire the fact that you did something."

"It wasn't selfless." The shame in his voice shocked me. "It wasn't as though I got nothing out of my years here. I can pretend it was noble, but in truth, she gave me something I needed, too."

"Acceptance?" I knew how desperate that need could feel.

He nodded. "No one else had ever wanted me as she did. And though I never stopped hating her, I began to need that. It sickens me to think of it now."

I stood and placed my napkin on the table, then walked slowly toward him as though approaching a wounded animal. I stopped just outside the reach of his claws. "I'm sorry that you're hurting, and I understand why you'd want to leave. But I think the city will be worse off without you."

His lips curled in a rueful half smile. "Because I save libraries?"

"More than that. You saved my life. You led your people to victory, even if they aren't thanking you for it. I think you're wiser than you give yourself credit for. You take chances to try to help others." I paused, then decided that I could be as honest as he had been. "I wish I could be more like that, but I get so scared of the consequences."

His eyes met mine, and for the first time I noticed the way the green irises were faintly marbled through with icy blue. Not human, after all, and absolutely spellbinding.

"Maybe you could take more chances as you find your place in this new world." His fingers curled, as though he was fighting the urge to touch me. "Regrets are hard, but I suspect that never opening yourself to possibilities is worse."

I had to look away. My gaze fell to his lips, soft curves that didn't quite match the hard lines of his jaw. Fascinating lips. The room seemed to grow warmer.

I squeezed my eyes closed. I couldn't think about him that way, no matter how kind he was, how weirdly attractive he might be, or how curious I was about what those claws might feel like on my skin.

When I opened my eyes, he'd stepped back a pace. My stomach clenched with disappointment. *Make up your mind, Hazel.*

"Thank you for a lovely evening," he said, his warm voice filling the space his body had vacated. He watched me intently. Seeing, I suspected, more than I'd have liked, but not taking advantage of my confusion. "It's been a long time since I found myself this comfortable speaking with someone. You must be tired, though. Shall I walk you to your room?"

"Thank you."

It was a good thing this monster was also a gentleman. Uncomfortable as I was with risks, I had to admit to myself that he was tempting.

I smiled as I remembered the first time I saw him. The devil, indeed. A convenient scapegoat for bad decisions since forever.

"What's so funny?" he asked.

"Nothing."

We didn't speak as we walked, and I didn't look out the windows we passed, where distant flames flickered against the black, star-filled sky. I stopped outside Verelle's rooms.

"This was lovely," I said. My heart fluttered into my throat as I realized how close he was standing. Not a friendly distance. Just far enough that he could look me over again, eyes lingering on the bare skin between my breasts and on my throat.

He looked hungrier than seemed decent for a perfect gentleman, but I could deal with that imperfection. His gaze met mine, and my heart stumbled.

I leaned back against the door. *He's going to kiss me. Do monsters even kiss here? Do humans? Or is it like the salute, completely different?*

Familiar, tingling warmth filled my body, electric currents that woke me up and brought the world into sharp focus, relaxing and exciting me at the same time.

Zinian placed one hand flat on the rough stone wall beside me and leaned closer.

I closed my eyes.

And yelped as the door opened and I tumbled into the room, saved from falling by Auphel's hand around my waist.

"Sorry!" she cried, and set me awkwardly on my feet. "I heard you and thought maybe I'd accidentally locked you out." Her eyes went wide as she spotted Zinian, and her lower lip trembled. "So sorry, sir."

She slammed the door, leaving us alone again.

Zinian laughed quietly. "Well. Goodnight, Hazel. We'll have to do this again before I leave."

As my head cleared from the shock, a queasy feeling came over me. I liked him. And when I loosened my hold on ideas of what should be allowed, I understood that I wanted him, monster or not. But getting involved with Zinian—with any monster, but especially one so powerful— was a bad idea. For both of us, if I'd interpreted his story correctly. But standing so close to him messed with my thoughts and instincts in ways I didn't understand, clouding them with physical desires.

Besides, I still had too many questions about the things he hadn't volunteered to talk about. Something niggled in the depths of my mind, something about him I didn't feel comfortable with, but it refused to come forward.

Always look before you leap. It's not worth the risk.

I reached behind me and opened the door.

"Thank you," I said as I stepped back, leaving him standing in the hallway looking bemused.

I closed the door behind me and leaned against it until my heart slowed. For the first time in my life, I couldn't tell whether the fluttering was from excitement or anxiety.

"How was supper?" Auphel asked. She'd retreated to her sleeping space by the cold hearth.

"I actually have no idea."

10

The next afternoon, I was ready to move out of the palace. The library had turned out to be a mess, but I was excited to get started on reshelving and reorganizing—not to mention have the opportunity to shut the world out for a while. The sight of real-life monsters roaming the palace halls had become familiar enough that their appearances no longer shocked me, but I still didn't care for the way most of them looked at me.

Auphel followed me down the palace halls, stopping when I paused to try the skeleton key in every locked door we passed. I hadn't had any luck so far. The key didn't even fit in any of the locks.

I was idly wondering what I would do if it did work, considering what I might find on the other side—A royally pissed-off Verelle? The wrong world?—when the key slipped neatly into a lock with a quiet click.

My heart skipped.

"Auphel," I whispered, and she stepped closer.

I hesitated. There were people I'd need to say goodbye to. Well, one person. Just to not seem rude, of course. I'd hardly been thinking about him, or our talk, or our almost-kiss. In fact, I sometimes made it ten whole minutes without him crossing my mind—before reminding myself that searching for romance here was a terrible idea. It was too scary. Even without the physical differences that should have made me question the whole thing, stepping into the spotlight by entering a relationship with someone as visible as him wouldn't bring the kind of attention I needed. It felt unsafe. Like a leap I wasn't ready to make.

Just go.

I turned the key.

Nothing moved. The door remained locked.

I let out my breath. "False alarm."

We'd reached the end of the long hallway that contained the bathing rooms. *At least I tried.* I tucked the key into the surprisingly utilitarian leather satchel I'd found in a trunk of Verelle's things. I supposed even an evil queen had to consider practicality sometimes.

We made our way through halls full of doors I'd already tried. Voices drifted out from one door that stood slightly ajar.

"—don't care where you put her," growled a familiar, feline voice, "as long as it means you'll keep your distance."

"I'm capable of deciding—"

"You're not. And it reflects badly on me as well as on you. I say this as a friend."

"I know." The door opened and Zinian stepped out. He stopped short, and Jaid slipped out behind him. I expected her to shoot me a dirty look and prowl away, but she stood with arms crossed and eyes narrowed, watching.

Auphel took a step away from them and averted her eyes, chewing her lip nervously, but she stayed close.

"Good afternoon, Hazel," Zinian said, sounding entirely friendly. If they were talking about me, it didn't seem to have bothered him. "I was just about to come looking for you. All ready to go?"

"I think so. I don't have much to move, but I guess I'll take some of the clothes from here."

"If you like," he said. "But I've found someone who once worked as a seamstress in a town south of here. She's accustomed to fitting humans, if you want some more practical clothing."

I hesitated. "I would love that, so much. But I'd feel terrible if it would be unpleasant for her."

His eyes crinkled at the outer corners, though he didn't quite smile. "That's kind of you. But Qinwan is currently making clothing for monsters, and is willing to use her considerable natural talents to help you, as well. Payment is taken care of, of course. My gift to you."

My cheeks warmed. "Then I accept. And thank you."

Jaid's tail whipped the air behind her. "Zinian, General Grys is expecting you. Best not to keep him waiting."

"Right." He sighed. "Hazel, perhaps we could dine at your new home once you've settled in? I'd like to discuss your findings as you go through the books."

"That would be nice," I said. "Thank you."

Zinian smiled and left us.

Jaid stayed behind. Auphel took a protective step closer to me. Jaid looked her over, then at me. "Stay away from him," she said. "Cancel those plans."

I took a deep breath. "Isn't that up to him?"

Her lips flared slightly. "I won't allow him to sabotage his own progress. He's worked hard for years to overcome his association with Verelle, but being seen with you will make things impossibly difficult for him." Her whiskers twitched, and she sighed. "Zinian is my friend, the best I've ever had. I have great respect for him, but the fact is that his years here in the palace warped him. He's not thinking straight. You seem like a reasonable human, which is rare enough that I'll trust you to do the right thing. Leave him to the monsters. Let him finish finding his place and establishing his role as a leader. If you become involved, you will destroy all of the progress he's made."

She flexed the short fingers of one hand, and sharp claws emerged. She used one to pick at her impressive fangs. A chill came over me. "You're safer if you stay away from him. Trust me. And do think about taking Grys up on his offer to send you away, once your little project is finished. For your own sake, if not for Zinian's. Find a mate of your own kind."

I was still struggling to form a response when she left us. The implied threat pissed me off. But that didn't mean she was wrong. An empty pit formed in my stomach, gnawing at me.

God, woman, get a grip. I was acting like the stupid, inconstant women I so hated in bad romance novels. It was as though there were two versions of me fighting an excessively dramatic battle over my words and actions. The me who liked and wanted to be with him, and the self that knew it was a terrible idea. I was terrified to think that something could happen between us, something that would open me to being hurt again. Every sign pointed to getting involved with Zinian being a bad idea. Jaid's words were just the final piece of the puzzle.

It hurt, but a sense of overwhelming relief flooded me. I was being rational. I was in control of my body and my emotions. He would understand, of course. We could work together, and be friends. It was a good plan. A safe plan.

My stomach churned. All of my rationalizations couldn't hide the fact that I was chickening out, plain and simple. Running away from risks and potential pain, just as I always did.

So fucking typical.

I gathered a few dresses from Verelle's room and slipped the religious text I'd found on my first day into my bag for later reading. It looked far older than any of the books I'd seen in the library or the palace, and worth preserving. I doubted Verelle's things would last long once the monsters were free to do as they pleased in there.

We met Zinian again as we left the palace. He was speaking to an armoured giant near the gate, who had crouched low to listen. The giant stood, and Zinian came toward us. He relaxed visibly and brightened as he walked toward me, which under other circumstances would have been a pleasant sight.

You made your decision. Pull up your big girl panties and deal with it.

He'd made his intentions clear the other night, when he almost kissed me. I'd have to be clear about my own now, before things got more complicated.

"Need a hand?" he asked.

"Um. Actually…"

I glanced at Auphel, who stepped back as Zinian came closer. She always leapt to obey him, but never acted like she was comfortable around him. Almost fearful, at times.

Something clicked almost audibly into place in my mind, and I understood what it was that had made me uncomfortable about Zinian since my first morning at the palace. He seemed genuinely kind and was certainly charming, but there was another side to him. One that I'd forgotten among everything else that had happened, or that had perhaps been drowned beneath my stupid attraction to him.

The night we'd met, Auphel had been ordered to kill me. This sweet, gentle giant who I couldn't imagine hurting a fly had been conscripted into the army, broken in body and spirit until she fit their twisted needs, and forced to commit violence.

And it wasn't just that she happened to be taken for the army. *Zinian* had chosen her. Auphel had said so herself. He'd taken her from her family when she was too young to know how to object. No wonder she shied away now as he approached, why she didn't look directly at him. She was afraid, but had nowhere to run. She couldn't even talk about it.

Suddenly I felt disgusted with myself for finding shelter under his wing, trusting him with my words, eating supper with him, falling under his spell.

What had the old book in my bag said about the true monster? *Fair of face and black of heart, with words of honey and claws of poison. Beware.*

I might not have believed in the book, but that was sound advice. I had ignored it once before, and look where that had got me. Jake had seemed too good to be true, but I'd ignored the anxieties that had tried to save me from a broken heart. I wasn't going to let that happen again.

Besides, I didn't only have myself to think about. I had my dear friend to consider, and not for anything would I fall for someone who had so hurt her. My body tensed as my nervousness turned to anger, and thoughts of keeping him in my life evaporated in its heat.

At least this made the decision easy, if not pleasant.

I hardened myself to his broad smile and tried not to think about the fact that I would be losing a powerful ally who understood my situation. There really were more important things.

At least speak to him, let him down easy. Show him that much kindness, after everything he's done for you.

"Hazel? You want help?"

"No, thank you," I said, realizing I'd been staring into space. I tried to smile and couldn't. "Auphel can handle my things, and we'll want to get back to work on the library. I'll be busy for a while, so it's probably best for both of us if I just focus on that."

"I see." And I thought he did. Completely. He straightened his shoulders and met my eyes squarely. His jaw tightened. "So we'll postpone supper plans, then?"

"Yeah." He didn't say anything, and the silence quickly became unbearable. "Thank you again for everything," I added. Even if I'd chosen Auphel over him, even if there was a sort of relief in letting go of him and having anger to lean into instead of passion, I didn't hate him. I couldn't. "For saving my life. Getting me a place in the city. I appreciate your kindness."

And it was true. He'd been more generous than I'd had any right to expect, especially given what it was costing him to associate with me. How could someone so nice be the kind of person who made a child fight in a war? But then, I'd never known anyone who turned out to be exactly what he seemed. We all show the world what we want it to see.

And we all make mistakes. But that mistake wasn't mine to forgive. It was Auphel's, and she was clearly still hurt.

At least I didn't feel like I was chickening out anymore. This was the best plan. I reached into my pocket and gave the skeleton key a squeeze, but didn't feel any comfort or sense of good luck in the gesture.

He placed a hand on his chest and bowed slightly. Before he looked away, I caught the pained look in his eyes. "You are most welcome. And I thank you for your part in ridding the world of Verelle, however unintentional it was. Let me know if you need me."

He didn't sound like he expected me to do that, but I nodded.

Auphel shifted my dresses from one arm to the other and started off toward the library. I followed and didn't look back.

Auphel and I fell into a comfortable routine as the next month passed, and I settled into my new life in the city. The seamstress came as promised, though I had heard no more about her from Zinian. She turned out to be a deer-headed woman named Qinwan with nimble fingers and a quick wit, and we found we got along quite well. She helped me with my clothing situation, creating sturdy pants and fitted shirts that suited me better than the gauzy gowns, taking the waists in a little when hard physical work and the healthier food of Elurien made it necessary. She also found me absorbent cloth when my time of the month hit, and I found myself wishing I had read more crazy adventure stories to see how anyone ever dealt with this sort of thing. Qinwan accompanied me to the market a few times, which was slowly being re-established by the monsters.

In fact, most of the city was getting back on its feet quite nicely with its new inhabitants. Qinwan's business was steadily growing. So were those of the candlemaker, the leather-worker (who created hard-soled slippers for me out of buttery leather), the butcher, and the farmers who brought goods to market. Money lingered, but bartering was making its way into the local economy. I heard all about the difficulties that were arising, but it seemed like things would only get better for the monsters. I still didn't go out alone, but the residents of the city were beginning to accept me, to understand that I was no part of the old threat.

I'd made the little apartment on the second floor of the library my own. The space was tucked under the peaked roof, and though it had only one room plus a bathroom, it was plenty for me. Auphel chose a space for herself downstairs in what had once been a storage room and kept it dark and cave-like, as pleased her ogrish sensibilities. She'd grown calm and tranquil as she settled into the idea that she didn't have to fight anymore—and since she no longer saw Zinian and the other military types.

Auphel and I occasionally ventured outside of the city walls and collected wildflowers from vast and colourful meadows that buzzed with bees and brightly coloured fairies. I cooked my meals in the kitchen, and Auphel kept me well supplied with firewood that she brought from the forest when she went on her personal hunting and gathering trips. We spent our days sorting through books and shelving them, trying to get a handle on hundreds of years of knowledge that was foreign to both of us. It was cozy, quiet, and after a time felt completely normal.

One sunny afternoon, Auphel decided to wander the city. I was happy to let her go alone. We were trying not to become too isolated from the city's inhabitants, but I was usually content to let them come to me if I had the choice. There were a few scholars who were already stopping in to inquire about and borrow books, and they seemed willing enough to accept me once I proved myself useful.

But today the library was quiet, and I felt like nesting, revelling in the dim quiet of my new home, and trying to forget my early days in Elurien. I knew I should be out trying doors, but had begun to slack off as time passed. It wasn't working, and the need to leave felt less urgent with each day that passed and each smile from strange new acquaintances.

It was becoming comfortable, but not everything felt settled.

I hadn't run into Zinian on the streets, though I watched for him. I wanted to know he was okay, and once I'd calmed down, I'd decided that I'd ask about Auphel if I saw him again. I didn't want to ask her and poke at old wounds she was obviously so reluctant to expose, especially when she was so happy in our new life. But maybe he would answer me. At least then I'd know his side of the story, and whether I'd been too hasty in my judgement.

I pushed away thoughts about him as they arose. *You did the right thing. He's better off without you, just like Jaid said. Find something else to focus on.*

I found a copy of the humans' religious text—titled the *Verhumn*—and carried it to a plush window seat to read. Beautiful as Verelle's copy was, I felt like the ancient pages were going to crumble under my fingers every time I touched them. This one was newer, larger, and written on thicker paper in dark ink.

I wasn't about to convert to these horrid people's beliefs, but I wanted to understand. I wanted to know why they thought themselves so much better than the monsters. If there was such a thing as the spark that Auphel had spoken about, a thing that sounded very much like my definition of a soul, then the monsters I'd met all had it in abundance.

The later pages were devoted to stories of the Great Mother Maela aiding the humans in subduing the monsters. Line drawings showed the monsters bowing gratefully before humans who glowed with what I assumed was their spark. Verelle's name came into it many times, detailing how the Mother had blessed her with the greatest spark so that she might lead them to victory against the monsters who refused to kneel. It turned my stomach. *History is written by the victors,* I reminded myself, and couldn't remember who had said it.

I almost regretted saving this trash from the fire. Though I'd found plenty of books full of good and useful information, this one was a black mark against those who had read and followed it.

I turned the pages backward. *And in those days the monsters roamed the land, living as animals, without understanding. The humans came among them, bearing the bright and divine spark bestowed upon them by divine grace. And the Mother decreed that men should rule over the beasts, and that the beasts would find the Mother's favour by submitting their wills to those of the spark-bearers, the humans.*

And there it was. The grounds for hundreds of years of slavery and servitude, all built on this passage. It sounded familiar, at least in part. I'd read this in Verelle's rooms. And yet—

The front doors burst open, flooding the dark library with light. Auphel entered, panting.

"Zinian is missing."

I slammed the book closed and coughed at the dust cloud that puffed out of it. "What?"

"I mean, he's gone. Jaid doesn't know where he is. Neither does the general, and they've been looking for him for days. Have you seen him?" Her eyes were as wide as I'd ever seen them, and her fingers twitched nervously. I went to her and laid a hand on her muscular back to calm her.

"I haven't seen him in weeks," I reminded her gently.

"Oh, right," Auphel sighed. She sat on the floor, cross-legged. It put her almost at eye-level with me. "I was hoping maybe you'd kept seeing him, even if you couldn't let anyone know. In secret, like. He seemed happy when he looked at you. Jaid wasn't wrong about things, but…" She shrugged. "I just wondered."

I leaned against a polished wood table and frowned—not at Auphel, but at this sudden shift from what I'd assumed she felt toward him. My chest tightened. "Why are you so loyal to him after what he did to you?"

Her brow furrowed. "After what?"

"After he took you from your family to serve in his army. After everything you went through there, after the way they used you and broke you." I nodded at her bad leg. "Anyone with a weaker spirit than yours would have been destroyed."

She reached out a finger to trace the patterns on the brightly coloured tile floor. "I don't like to talk about it."

"I remember."

She nodded slowly, frowning down at her hands. "But I will if you won't ever tell anyone."

"Of course I won't." I sat on the cold floor with her.

"I owe Major Zinian an awful lot." She took a deep breath. "Do you remember the ogre who was there when you were going to be sent away? Kringus?"

"I do." He'd seemed a horrible, nasty brute. "Someone you know well?"

"He could have been. He came to my parents and asked to take me as his mate. He'd noticed my strength, and thought me beautiful. I didn't want to go. He frightened me. He still does. But my parents said I had to. They had too many mouths to feed, and he was a good connection for them to have. I ran into the woods, crying, but there was nothing I could do."

"God, Auphel. That's horrible."

She sighed. "He would not have been kind to me. No better than his first three mates. None of them lived too long. So I hoped and wished that something would happen to him. That he would fall into the lake and sink forever, that the humans would take him or he would be killed in the war my parents talked about. Anything to get me out of him coming to collect me. And one night there was a knock at the door, loud and hard. I expected Kringus, but it was Zinian and some of his soldiers. I crept out of my sleeping hole and stood in the corner while they talked about taking my brothers to fight, and me too. My parents argued that I wasn't old enough or trained at all, but Zinian knew about Kringus. He said…" Her cheeks flushed. "He said if I was old enough to… mate… I was old enough to fight."

I suspected that wasn't the word he'd used, but nodded for her to go on.

"My parents agreed to let me go. I think Zinian would have taken me even if they hadn't. I hated everything about being in the army, but it was better than Kringus." She wiped a finger under her nose. "And a few years into the fighting, I got up the nerve to ask Zinian why he'd fought to take me when he could have just had my brothers. They were all bigger and stronger and good fighters. I was so bad at it, and pretty useless."

"And?" I asked around the lump in my throat. I thought I knew what she was going to say, and felt ill over the mistake I'd made.

"Zinian did a lot of scouting, because he was looking for special kinds of soldiers. He'd seen me crying after the decision about the mating, and he knew what Kringus was like. He said he couldn't stop Kringus directly, but he could recruit me. I was safer as a soldier than as a mate, see. He thanked me for working so hard to become a valuable part of the army, and said he saw something special in me. That he knew I had an important part to play. It made me feel important, you know?" A tear slipped out of her eye. "Since then I've tried not to let him down."

"Then why are you afraid of him?"

Her cheeks flushed. "He makes me nervous, I guess. He's powerful and important. It makes me feel funny when I get special attention from those kinds of people. It's scary."

"Well, shit." I stood and paced the library as shame and regret battled for top position in my mind. "And you have no idea where he is?" I wasn't worried about him, but wanted more than anything to apologize. I'd been the asshole in this situation. I'd rejected him when he thought he'd found someone who wouldn't judge him for his appearance or his ideas. Hell, I'd rejected the only person who wouldn't avoid me because of mine. All because I had jumped to a stupid conclusion about a once-frightening warrior and been spooked by my own too-quick feelings for him.

I thought back over our brief association, the kindness and acceptance he'd showed me, the connection I'd felt with him in spite of our outward differences, the pain in his eyes when I'd turned away from him. My chest tightened painfully, and I let regret settle in. I didn't deserve to be spared it.

Dumbass. I really was no better than some stupid girl in a romance.

"Not one clue where he went," Auphel said. "Jaid said not to trouble myself about it, but I'm worried. He's been in such a low mood, but I thought maybe you were helping with that."

"Let me think." He'd said he wasn't going to stay in the city, so this wasn't surprising. What did concern me was the fact that he apparently hadn't even told Jaid where he was going. They were friends. If anyone should have known where he was, it was her. I thought back to the night we'd dined together. He'd spoken of hunting in the woods and the harpy who had raised him. Nothing else that might help, but it was a start.

"Do you know where he grew up?" I asked.

She squinted. "Sort of. Alandra raised him, and she comes from the cliffs above the hidden forest. But I'm sure Grys checked there."

"Hmm. But maybe he didn't want Grys to find him. We're not Grys."

Auphel perked up at that. "You think he'd come out for us?"

"I don't know." If the hurt look on his face when I'd said goodbye to him last time was any indication, he might not want to see me. "All we can do is try. At least then you'll know he's okay."

She nodded. "I hope he's not lonely. Alandra killed herself when she felt her work was done with him, of course." She said this as though it was unfortunate, but not unusual.

"Sorry, what?"

Auphel shrugged. "Harpies are strange. They don't like outsiders bothering them, or even letting nature take control. They kill themselves when they think their work is done and their best years over. Better than wasting away, or something."

And I thought I was a control freak.

"I think Alandra would have done it a lot sooner if she hadn't had a baby dumped in her nest." Auphel wrinkled her nose. "Disgusting creatures, but they pay their debts. They're proud about punishing themselves for their mistakes and wrong-doings." She saw the horrified look on my face and quickly added, "Zinian's not like them, though."

Nature or nurture. He'd said he felt useless, that his work was done. What had he said to me when I dismissed him? *Let me know if you need me.*

I didn't think he'd let go over something as silly as a human's rejection. Still, I raced upstairs to pack as quickly as I could.

11

An hour later I was riding piggy-back on an ogre as she raced through a sun-dappled forest, water skins flopping under her arms as her crooked gait carried us toward the desert she assured me wasn't too far away. In fact, we ended up camping at the edge of that forest, at the sharp line where the white sands of the desert began. I didn't see any sign of cliffs, but Auphel assured me they were there.

"See the piles of rocks in the distance? That's where we're going."

"That's so far!"

She leaned back on her elbows and reached out with a long stick to poke the campfire we'd built. "You leave that to me, tiny person."

As the sunlight vanished millions of stars appeared, spilling across the sky in a display more spectacular than anything I'd ever seen at home. I'd never been one for camp-outs. I hadn't realized what I was missing.

We set out early the next morning to get in as much travel as we could before the sun fully rose, but the rocks never seemed to get any closer. By mid-morning we both reeked of sweat, and I felt faint from the heat. Auphel carried me without complaint across the low dunes, and I urged her to drink most of the water. She followed a road hidden beneath a thin layer of sand that allowed her to keep her speed up, but the exertion had to be brutal. I closed my eyes against the white glare and tried to rest.

I didn't open them again until Auphel slowed hours later. She stumbled forward, and I hit the ground with a thud. Not on sand, but on grass.

"Sorry," she mumbled. "We're here."

I stood and brushed bits of greenery from my pants, then dropped my bag to the ground. "I'll be damned."

We'd reached the rocks, a trio of massive boulders on top of a lump of red stone that hunched out of the ground higher than my head. They crowned a wide gorge that had been completely hidden at a distance. We stood at the narrow end of the gap, which broadened as it sloped downward. The steep, grassy slope led down into a lush forest where the tops of the trees sat well below the level of the desert. Vines twisted through the deciduous branches, creating a tangled canopy so thick I was tempted to try walking on it. Auphel led the way below, climbing carefully over rocky outcroppings and loose stones.

I followed her into the cool, moss-scented darkness of the forest. It took some time for my eyes to adjust after the brightness of the desert, and for a few minutes I felt blind, surrounded by shadows filled with mysterious creaks and chattering noises. The forest world came slowly into focus, wild and frightening. Something crashed through the trees far to our left, and I moved closer to Auphel.

The leaves rustled in the breeze that reached them from above, but all was calm and still below. I heard the river before I saw it, and thirst I'd nearly forgotten about came rushing back as the water came into view.

"Is it safe to drink?" I asked Auphel. I unstuck my shirt from my sweaty skin. "Or to swim in?"

"Both," she said. "But don't get swept away. This river comes from and leads to underground caves. You don't want to get lost in there."

I slipped into the water fully clothed, and wished I'd packed soap. I'd be quite the sight if we found Zinian. But then, I suspected I'd ruined any chance of romantic notions on his part. I only hoped he'd hear my apology and agree to be friends. In this world, we were both judged harshly for our appearances. But we could stick together, tell each other that it didn't matter.

If he wanted to be alone, I would let him. I just wanted him to know he didn't have to be.

The river was cold, but not as bad as I would have expected from something that flowed from the depths of the world. That thought led to wondering what sorts of things might live down there and whether they were ever swept up here by the current, and I washed a little more quickly. Much as I was enjoying getting clean and hydrated, I wasn't keen on having my legs chomped by strange monsters. I dunked my hair and washed the sand and dust and sweat out, then slipped out of my clothes and wrung them out underwater, scrubbing the dirtiest bits against the rocks.

Auphel joined me in the water and floated on her back. I grabbed her ankle as she drifted downstream, and she laughed. "Ogres taste terrible," she said. "The ground would spit me out if it swallowed me."

"Let's not test that."

I climbed out of the river and sat on a rock while the air dried me, then put my spare clothes on and spread the wet ones out to dry on a bush. Auphel hadn't brought extras, so she just wore hers out of the water and dripped everywhere.

"Where to now?" I asked, after a quick meal of dried fruit and meat.

"This way."

The gorge had widened considerably, and it took us a while to reach the stone walls. They rose straight up from the forest, smooth and beautiful, covered in rippling marbled stripes of cream and crimson. Auphel set her hands on her hips.

"There's a path, but it's too narrow for me."

I followed her gaze and swallowed hard as my stomach clenched. Not a path, exactly, but a small ledge that climbed the wall, twisting back on itself as it rose. There, high up on the wall, was the dark opening of a cave.

"You're joking."

"If he came home, that's where we'll find him."

He must really want to be alone, I thought. *Maybe we shouldn't disturb him...*

No. I needed to know he wasn't there, wasn't lonely or hurt or worse. No more letting my fears make my decisions for me, no more running away when things got intense. I squared my shoulders and hoisted myself up onto the small ledge where the path ended, then pressed my back against the wall and shuffled sideways.

"Don't look down!" Auphel called.

I looked ahead instead, and stepped carefully over the washed out parts of the path. I swept loose stones out of my way with my foot and tried to ignore the increasing duration of the clattering noises they made as they fell. The first switchback almost made me give up, but I held my breath and stepped up onto the next level.

If there was ever a time to start praying, this would be it. But I had no interest in the Mother of this world if she made people into what the humans had become. I'd have to make it alone.

I kept moving. Check, shuffle, clear the path, shuffle, up to the next level. I had no idea how much time might be passing. I looked up to see how much farther I had to go. Not much compared to how far I had to have come, but the cave opening was still several body lengths above me.

My foot slipped. My heart lurched as I pressed my back harder against the wall and scrambled to find something to grab onto. Rocks and loose soil skittered down the face of the cliff as my right foot dangled over open air. The muscles in my left thigh screamed as they held me up, half-crouched. I forced myself to stand, waited until my heart slowed and the white spots in front of my eyes cleared, then checked the path ahead and stepped over the gap.

Only then did I realize how stuck I'd be if there wasn't another way down.

Go down now. At least you know the path is safe that way.

But the top was closer, and I needed to rest my legs and my aching hands. *And Zinian might be there. Just a little more.*

A few minutes that seemed like eternities later, I flopped belly-first onto the small ledge that jutted out from the cave entrance. I got to my knees and turned to look down. The forest stretched out below me, verdant and lush, and the breeze that swept over it and past the cave held the metallic scent of the river. I breathed deep and waited for the tremors in my legs to stop before I stood and stepped into the cave.

I didn't see him until my eyes adjusted to the gloom, and the sight startled me. Zinian stood still as the stone walls that surrounded us, arms crossed over his bare chest, watching me. His face was a mask, showing neither surprise nor pleasure at seeing me.

I brushed the dust off my pants and realized I'd completely ruined the effects of my bath. Exertion and panic had coated my body with a fresh layer of sweat, and my still-damp hair lay in tangles over my shoulders. "How long have you been standing there?" I asked.

"I heard you and Auphel down below."

I gritted my teeth. "And you didn't think to come down to greet us?"

His expression didn't change. "I didn't ask you to come. I didn't ask Grys' men to come, either, and I didn't come out to greet them when they called for me. I wish to be alone." He stepped forward, and for a second I thought he was going to shove me off the cliff. Instead he motioned for me to come deeper into the shadows.

"Why didn't you tell anyone you were leaving?" I asked.

"Because I'm not a captive in that city anymore, but I still feel like one. The only way I can prove my freedom to myself is to come and go as I please, without notice or permission. Why are you here?"

I rested against the cool stone wall and looked around. We were in a cave made up of smooth curves, like it had been carved out by wind or water. There was no furniture, no source of light save for the cave's entrance.

I met Zinian's eyes. I wanted to chicken out, to say it was nothing and maybe just toss myself onto the breeze to avoid making a fool of myself, but I owed him this. "I came to apologize."

He raised an eyebrow, but said nothing.

"I'm sorry for pushing you away. You're one of few people who was kind to me when I got here, and I..." I hesitated. "I took some advice that seemed good. I thought it would be better for you if you weren't seen with me." I wanted to leave it at that, but forced myself onward. "And I was scared, because I like you. A lot. I um… I find you quite interesting, and I feel…"

Dammit. Though I hadn't read many romances, I was fully aware that the big speech was supposed to sound a lot better than this. I skipped ahead to the most important part.

"I thought you had hurt Auphel. Then she explained to me how you helped her by taking her for your army. Saved her, really. All I knew before was that you took a child away from her family to fight, and I thought you were—"

"A monster?" He smiled sadly. "You weren't wrong. I've done more than my share of questionable things in my quest to bring Verelle down and gain my freedom. We have our victory, but the cost has been high for so many. I'm not a hero, Hazel, and I have many regrets."

"I'm starting to accumulate a few, myself. I'm so sorry if I hurt you."

"I've had far worse injuries than this." He stretched his wings out behind him, and I couldn't help staring at the way it made the muscles of his torso move. Tough and lean. Carved by war. Not exactly the carefully sculpted human ideal of my world, and better by leagues. "So that's all? You wanted to apologize?"

"Yes. Well, and ask you to supper. I owe you a good meal."

He chuckled and stepped closer. "I accept. You're cooking this time."

"Fair." My voice squeaked out. He didn't say anything else, and the silence between us grew heavy. "I really am sorry."

"You said that."

"I know. I'm blabbering because I have no idea what to do." A smile touched his eyes, which glimmered with their own faint light in the dark cave. My mouth went dry. I looked down, focusing on the scars that crisscrossed his chest. "I do like you. In a lot of ways. And that scares me more than anything else has since the night I got here."

"I know. It frightens me, too." He reached out and traced a claw along the line of my jaw. I shivered. There was no threat there, but the strange sensation thrilled me. He cupped my face in his hand, which was so much warmer than the cool tones of his skin hinted at, and tilted my chin up.

"We could skip the meal," he whispered.

My knees turned liquid, and I pressed harder against the wall so I wouldn't crumple to the floor. "We could."

I stepped forward as he leaned in, and our lips met, hard and fast. He pulled back slightly, and I felt his mouth curve into a smile as I put my hand behind his neck to pull him in again. His touch sent thick desire coursing through my body. I'd wanted people before, but never in a way that felt this irrational and wild.

It seemed that monsters *did* kiss. And quite well, too.

I let my hands wander over his chest and then up to his face, tracing the ridges of the scars on his cheek. When I reached up to brush through his hair, my fingers knocked against one of his twisted horns.

It should have felt strange. It only made me want him more. Something about his monstrous nature had become twice as appealing to me as the beauty of his human parts.

If him wanting me was as warped as Jaid had said, I supposed I was at least as far gone as he was.

His hands roamed over my upper body, surprisingly gentle, until his claws pressed hard against my waist, piercing the fabric of my shirt and tearing it slightly. And still I wasn't afraid of him. The thought of those claws tracing over my bare skin whipped me into a frenzy.

He nipped my lower lip with a sharp canine tooth, and I gasped.

"Sorry," he murmured, without pulling back.

"Don't be." I pressed my hips against him. He was obviously as excited as I was, and for the first time I let myself wonder whether that part of him was more human or monster.

"Hazel!" Auphel bellowed from below, her voice slowly penetrating the haze that clouded my mind. "Hey!"

Zinian growled deep in his throat and stepped away, but his eyes never left me.

"Um, Hazel?" Auphel called again. "I need you. We're not alone, here."

Zinian's attention snapped to the cave entrance. "See what's going on," he said. "I need a minute."

I needed one, too, but my situation would be less obvious to bystanders. I went to the ledge, knelt, and peered over. Auphel stood at the base of the cliff, joined by the silver-furred form of Jaid and a black horse weighed down with weapons and water sacks.

Jaid looked up. "Did you find him, then?"

Zinian stepped forward and crouched beside me. "She did," he called down. "So kind of you to follow." He turned to me. "I'll come back for you. Don't try to follow me down."

He stood and spread his wings, then tipped off the edge. He flew a slow lap over the tops of the trees, wings catching the breeze, and looped down to speak with Jaid and Auphel.

I moved away from the edge and sat in the shadows. Looking down was making me queasy, and I needed a minute to catch my breath.

Zinian returned, landing neatly on the ledge outside, and stalked into the cave. He offered me a hand and pulled me to my feet. "We have to return to the city."

I would have been pleased to have him coming back with us if he hadn't appeared so distressed. "Why? What's wrong?"

His nostrils flared slightly as he looked toward the forest. "I don't know. The scholars who've been borrowing your books have learned something about Verelle's whereabouts. They want to see both of us. And they want your key."

A chill came over me. "Something bad?"

"I don't know. I doubt they'd have sent for me if it were good news. Come on, I'll take you down."

We stood at the edge of the cliff. "Put your arms around me," he said. "I can't fly carrying too much extra weight, but we can glide down."

My chest tightened. "You're sure?"

"I am. Actually…" He wrapped an arm under my butt and scooped me up. "Wrap your legs around my waist."

Not exactly how I was hoping to receive that order.

I held on tight as he leaned forward, and we fell.

12

We followed the palace corridors to the meeting room where the leaders had decided my fate.

The journey back had been long and uncomfortable. Auphel had carried me again while Jaid rode and Zinian flew, and I'd felt like the weakest link in the group. It was a wonder that creatures as comparatively frail as humans had risen up to rule this world. The night in the forest had been long and cold, and Jaid's sharp eyes and sharper tongue kept me and Zinian apart. I'd hardly slept until nearly dawn and had wakened feeling worse than when I'd closed my eyes.

All of that paled now as Jaid pushed the door open.

Three scholars waited for us. I recognized the elderly male centaur, with his pale coat and fluffy white hair, and the female minotaur whose slim human body seemed ill-equipped to hold up her bovine head.

The dog that sat between them was a stranger. It watched as we entered, shaggy black-and-white head cocked to one side, ears perked up.

The table was covered with leather- and cloth-bound books that made the room feel only slightly warmer than the last time I'd visited it.

"At last," the dog said, and rested a forepaw on the table. "We've been waiting."

"My apologies, Tuwina," Zinian said.

"You have the key?"

I took it from my bag. I was no longer using it as a lucky charm, but never went anywhere without it on the chance that I might find a locked door to try. "I haven't had any luck so far."

I handed it to Eriel, the minotaur. "You will," she said. "All of the information is here, encoded in these books. Tuwina has deciphered enough that we think we have found the door we need. And we believe we know where Verelle is, and how to bring her back to face justice—if that's what we decide is the proper course of action."

"Sit," the dog said. We obeyed. Zinian took the seat next to me and gave my hand a quick squeeze under the table.

"Is there any question that Verelle should be brought back?" he asked. "If we're ready for her, we can end it quickly." He didn't add that he'd finally be able to rest once it was done, but I heard it in the tightness of his voice. This was what he had lived for these past years, ever since he'd seen the depths of her cruelty. He would finally be free.

The scholars exchanged glances. "That will be up to the leaders, of course," Eriel said. "You among them, Zinian. We needed to speak to the human to be certain it would be possible." She turned her chocolate-brown eyes on me and blinked slowly. "Hazel, we understand you've wanted to go home."

"I have," I said with less certainty than I would have spoken with a few weeks before.

"Verelle is in your world. It seems that she didn't call you here, but she did use your arrival to her advantage. She saw an opening, and she made the exchange. We believe that because of that connection, returning you home would bring her here."

My heart lurched. "She's there? In my world? My town?"

"Not to worry," said Daun, the old centaur. "We're almost certain her magic would be useless there, if she's still alive."

"Almost?"

Daun and Eriel exchanged another look over Tuwina's head. "You said there's no magic in your world. We're not concerned," Tuwina said.

I let out a breath. At least there was that.

"All would be restored to what it was before," Eriel assured me.

My breath caught in my throat. That was what I'd hoped for, wasn't it? When I'd arrived in this world, all I'd wanted was to go home. But now… now things were different. If I wasn't in love with Zinian, I at least thought we were on our way to something that might be amazing, better than anything I'd had at home. I'd be leaving my dear Auphel, and Qinwan. And my library, which was beginning to feel like a real home. I'd be abandoning my work there, which had already turned out to be so helpful. And to return to what? A critical mother and a hen-pecked father, at least until I saved enough money to move to my own shabby little place. A life surrounded by the same people I'd tried to leave behind once before. A world that was familiar and comfortable, but that I could only picture in black and white after the excitement and colour of this one.

I could have been happy here, I realized, and my throat tightened. It would have been so hard, but so worth it. In Elurien I might have learned to let go of my fears, to take chances and be the new person I already felt myself becoming.

But I couldn't leave my world to suffer under Verelle. Not if the scholars weren't completely certain that she wasn't harming my old friends and family. And not if it would keep this world from the resolution it so needed, and Zinian from finishing the task he'd taken up years ago.

I hadn't realized that everyone was staring at me until I finished thinking and raised my eyes to meet Tuwina's. "I suppose I should go, then."

"Wait," Zinian said. "Are we certain it's safe? What if Hazel opens a door and it's to the wrong world? What if something goes wrong, and we don't know to help her?"

Jaid's mouth opened in surprise. She had wanted him to give up his obsession with Verelle, but I doubted she'd be pleased by the concerns that had displaced it. They pleased me, though.

"We'll make sure we have all of the information we need before we do anything," Eriel said. "Hazel has become a member of our community, and we don't wish to see her harmed. Besides, accuracy is the only way to be certain that Verelle will be called back."

Auphel chewed the skin beside her thumbnail, but remained silent.

"We'll speak to the other leaders and finish our planning tonight," Daun said, reaching for a heavy book bound in rough hide. "We thank you all. You're excused."

I fought down the bile that rose in my throat. *This is how it should be,* I told myself, and remembered the stories of my childhood. Didn't people always have to go home at the end of these adventures? Dorothy did. Peter and Susan and what's-their-names did. Balance was always restored.

We rose to leave. All except Auphel. "You're sure it has to be this way?" she asked.

"We are," Daun said, not unkindly. "We are terribly sorry."

Zinian leaned over Auphel's shoulder. "I'll see that you stay on to work in the library," he said. His voice held a rough edge, and he spoke quietly.

Auphel nodded and stood. "Thank you. That wasn't what I was worried about, though."

We stepped into the hallway, and Jaid cleared her throat. "This is a good thing you're doing, Hazel." She offered a hand, and I shook it. "If I don't see you again, I wish you well."

I smiled uncertainly. "Thanks."

She turned and left.

"I'll see you at the library?" Auphel asked.

"Sure."

Everything was crumbling around me already. My heart fluttered like a caged bird as I watched her shamble away. I closed my eyes.

Zinian placed a hand on my arm, and I leaned against the solid reality of his body. He rested his chin on top of my head and held me close.

"I don't want you to go," he said. "Much as I want to see Verelle's head roll, it's not worth losing you. You can change your mind."

"No," I said, and sniffled. I hadn't realized I was crying. "I want to stay here with you. But my people might be in danger. My whole world. I have to know."

"I understand." He let go, and I stepped away from him.

"So," I said, and made myself smile. "You still want to come by for supper? Last chance."

He didn't smile back. "I wouldn't miss it for anything."

13

Auphel grew restless that day, and decided to spend the night outside of the city, roaming the woods and sleeping under the stars as she'd done before my arrival. I understood the impulse. I couldn't stay still, myself, and wanted nothing more than to run from the inevitable goodbyes. She left early, and I spent the afternoon tidying the library, cleaning my apartment, and bathing and grooming myself as well as I could with nothing but a bar of soap and a hairbrush.

In a spare moment I tried to write a letter to Zinian explaining how I felt. I knew I wouldn't be able to say it out loud. The ink was lovely, the paper smooth, my penmanship perfect, and yet the words wouldn't come. I'd known kind and generous people before. I'd known attractive people before, and brave ones. I had cared for people and loved them. But it had never added up to this. This strange feeling that I wanted to protect him even as I wanted to let him do the same for me, that I wanted to feel his soul—his spark, maybe—as much as I wanted to feel his body, that losing him would hurt more than losing my entire old life had. I'd never so regretted needlessly losing time with someone, or felt so shattered at the thought of separation.

I wrote that and more, but my attempts came out sounding melodramatic and not at all like what I truly felt. I balled up the paper and put the ink away.

I should have been excited about going home, but everything around me was a reminder of what I was leaving behind. The cool quiet of the library, filled with the miraculously warm and living scent of books... the heavy woven blankets I'd found for my bed, patterned in a riot of pink and red roses, and the cool sheets beneath... even the cantankerous wood stove in my apartment nearly made me weep when I realized that I'd never enjoy its warmth on a winter evening while I snuggled in with a cup of sinsl, the fresh, sweet herbal tea blend Qinwan had introduced to me.

When I left to visit the butcher—on my own for the first time—I noticed that the monsters in the street no longer glared at me. They ignored me or gave curt but polite nods. They would have accepted me in time, I decided. Perhaps I could have helped them record their stories and history and kept all of it safe in the library. It would have been a massive undertaking, but fascinating. Tales of monsters and magic seemed quite appealing now that they were reality, and I could have collected them for barter. Memories for meat, stories for soap. A valuable service to offer.

But I only had one night, and I wasn't planning to spend it with paper and ink. I'd considered the fact that it would be easier to keep my distance now, and decided I would never forgive myself if I didn't make the most of every moment I had left with Zinian.

I dressed in a long skirt and a loose peasant-style blouse. Nothing underneath. Monsters didn't care much for undergarments, and I was getting used to it. Still, this fabric was thin enough that I felt half-naked in spite of the shirt's otherwise modest coverage.

I prepared two servings of meat in the cast-iron pan that the apartment's last inhabitant had left behind. I'd just set the meat out to rest and started on a plain salad of wild greens when the door opened.

"Smells good."

The hairs on the back of my neck prickled at his voice. "Not bad, right? I hope I didn't overcook it."

Zinian looked around the apartment, taking in the softly glowing candles, the framed prints of purple wildflowers on the wall, the huge window, and the wide bed with its single pillow and neatly folded blankets that I'd left turned down at the foot. "It's still exceedingly human," he said, running his fingers over a shelf that displayed a small collection of wooden toys I'd found in the library, "but I like it far better than the palace."

"So do I. That place is pretty, but so cold."

He hadn't bothered with a shirt this time. I supposed that was a formality that we'd moved beyond. I was glad. The less he was trapped by human things, the more comfortable he became. I watched as he moved with raw, powerful grace through my home, seeming to fill it with his presence even as he kept his wings tucked in close to avoid knocking into the furniture. His long talons clicked over the floor. I remembered how terrified I'd been when we'd met.

I couldn't say I wasn't scared now, but it was a far more pleasant feeling tonight. My skin tingled, and I became aware of every soft brush of my clothing against it.

He stopped near the overstuffed loveseat, but didn't sit. "It feels like you in here."

"It's getting there."

"You're sure you want to leave? Pull-toys and gaudy blankets are a lot to leave behind." His joking tone sounded forced and hard.

I left the food on the sideboard and went to him. "They're not what I'm sorry to be leaving."

His hands flexed at his sides as he looked up to take in the bare-beamed rafters overhead. "The plan seems too risky. You're safe here, now. Even Jaid is softening."

"Only because I'm going," I noted. "I don't think she'd be too happy about this."

"Good thing neither of us answers to her."

"Good thing." The food was getting cold, but I'd lost my appetite for it. "Everyone must be happy that this will all be over soon. That Verelle will get what she deserves."

Zinian's shoulders slumped. "Not so long ago, that thought would have thrilled me."

I stepped closer. "What thrills you now?"

He smiled slightly, revealing the barest hint of fangs. "You. The way we kissed in the cave. The fact that we're here together, and actually alone this time."

My cheeks warmed. I knew what I wanted. What would thrill me. I knew it was risky, that it would make leaving that much harder. Relationships with no future had never figured into my plans.

I didn't care. I needed to be reckless this once, to be brave and take something I wanted just because it felt right in the moment, never mind the consequences.

I traced the line of his jaw and trailed my fingers slowly over his throat and his chest, down the hard lines of his stomach. My body responded to the sight and smell of him, and the shirt I wore did nothing to hide it. He smiled slowly as he watched me, taking every detail in, as seemed to be his way.

I would miss being looked at like that.

Zinian shivered, but his voice when he spoke was thick and warm. "I really think we should skip supper."

He leaned in and kissed me far more gently than he had in the cave, lips barely brushing mine. I lifted myself onto my toes to get closer and placed my hands on his shoulders.

"I wish we had more time," he whispered, and kissed behind my ear. "I want to take this slowly enough to drive you insane."

I drew in a quick breath as he untucked my billowy blouse and explored the bare flesh beneath, trailing his claws over my back and my stomach, using the pad of his thumb to press gently against one nipple as he cupped my breast, moving slowly and with perfect control.

I gasped. "You are a monster, aren't you?"

"I did warn you."

He tried to pull the blouse over my head, but I stopped him. "Hang on. You first."

"Go ahead, then." He waited, hands hanging at his sides, the barest hint of a smile daring me to do as I wished.

I reached for the laces on his pants as though stripping a monster bare was the most natural thing in the world, loosened the strings, and eased them down over his finely shaped backside.

"Well?"

I nearly laughed with relief, but sensed that wouldn't go over well. "Impressive. Perfect. Is it all right for me to say I'm glad your human parent contributed that part?"

He chuckled. "Absolutely. Your turn, now."

I looked him over, wings to horns to claws, and hesitated.

"What?" he asked.

"I just… I won't be too human for you?"

He grabbed the hem of my shirt again. I lifted my arms over my head and closed my eyes. Though the air in the apartment was warm, a chill came over me as it caressed my skin. My skirt slipped easily over my hips and hit the floor.

I reminded myself that he wanted me as I was, that he would have thought razors and makeup and fancy underwear were ridiculous. Here, I just had to be me. But would it be enough?

"Hazel. Look at me."

I opened my eyes. He'd ducked his head down, placing his face before mine. My chest tightened and then seemed to liquefy as our eyes met.

"You are human. And you are beautiful. You are yourself, and all I want." His gaze travelled appreciatively over my body. "And you should never wear clothes."

I laughed, and he pulled me into a deep kiss. It seemed impossible that he should want me as badly as I wanted him. In that moment I thought I might be swept away on the waves of my own desire as they burned through my body.

Damn plans. Damn consequences.

I fell back on the bed and pulled him down with me. His wings spread as though to slow the fall, and remained flexed as he bent to trail kisses down my throat and over my chest. Every brush of his lips and tongue sent shudders through me, and the faint scratch of his teeth on my breast was nearly enough to push me over the edge. I grabbed his hair and pulled his face to mine. His teeth grazed my tongue, drawing blood, and I pulled him closer.

He propped himself up on one elbow and brushed my hair away from my face. Our eyes met, and my heart stilled.

I don't love him, I told myself. *I can't. It's too soon.* And yet the connection we shared felt deeper and wilder and more exciting than anything I'd known before. More promising.

I'd had to step into a fairy tale to find something real.

His claws trailed over my thighs, and I opened them to him. He touched me without scratching, again using the pads of his fingers, only teasing with his claws.

"Shit," I gasped.

He laughed, then caught something in my expression that made him pause. "What?"

"I just…" He didn't stop touching me as I spoke, and it made it hard to find the words. "I'm scared of falling for you more than I already have."

His smile returned, gentle and somehow devilish at the same time. He leaned in and kissed my throat.

"I don't want you to fall," he whispered as he rolled on top of me, teasing with gentle pressure. "I want you to fly."

I didn't let myself think about losing him, about never finding this again. Instead I lost myself in his eyes, in his body, in the relentless thundering of our hearts and the sound of his breath in my ear as we moved together.

I lost control. And for once, I didn't mind.

* * *

The sun shone far too brightly the next morning, and the birds flittering outside the window mocked me with their brilliant plumage and cheerful songs.

Zinian and I lay silent, facing each other, covers thrown aside. We'd run out of words and energy hours before, but I hadn't slept much. As the beginnings of faint sunlight breached the dark of our private space, I'd begun memorizing the lines of his face and his body.

Remembering would hurt, but forgetting would mean going back to sleep after something new had been awakened in me. I didn't want to forget the way my chest ached when I looked into his eyes, the way other parts of me stirred when he smiled at me. I'd always thought the idea that a person could fall in love so quickly was ridiculous. I'd certainly taken my cautious time about it before. But I suspected I'd found something in Zinian that defied logic or plans. A kindred soul of sorts. One who made me feel brave, who understood my wounds, who would accept my shadows along with my bright spots, just as I would his.

The people of my world would never understand what I'd sacrificed for them.

I touched my cold feet to the warm scales of his lower legs, and he trailed a long talon over my ankle.

His gentleness had come as a shock to me. Though he kissed forcefully, and he'd excited me with the threat of the physical power of his body, he'd put my pleasure before his and accommodated my weaker human form all night as though he couldn't have wished for anything else.

If my mattress had suffered at the mercy of his claws when he lost control, it was no great loss.

I wanted more. Wanted to know what else he was capable of. Wanted to know what he would be like if we had time to play, time to tease. What it would be like to let ourselves go without fear of ruining the only night we'd ever have together.

And yet… And yet it had been perfect.

Zinian pulled me closer. I tucked my head under his chin and breathed in the scent of his skin, wild and indescribably exciting. I wondered whether he carried the essences of every creature that had gone into making him.

He rolled me onto my back and slipped lower to nuzzle under my chin, nipping gently at the soft skin of my throat. "We could just stay here," he said, his voice barely a whisper, as though he was afraid to break the spell we'd woven together in our silence.

"Sure. No one would notice if I didn't show up." I lifted his face and pulled him in to kiss my lips.

For the last time.

No. There's time. We still—

A heavy fist pounded on the door in a familiar non-rhythm.

"Auphel," we said together. My insides fluttered in panic, and I fought the urge to hide under the bed.

I knew what I had to do. It was the right thing, the brave thing. And the absolute last thing I wanted.

I didn't let myself think of home in anything but the vaguest rose-tinted tones as Zinian and I dressed. My polka-dot pyjama pants were long gone, but I had pants and a shirt that would only look a little out of place until I found something else.

Zinian let Auphel in, and she ducked her head down to pass under the arched doorway. She sat on the floor. "Ready?" she asked.

"No."

They both looked at me, and tears prickled my eyes. "I'll never be ready, though. And I'll never have the right words to thank either of you for what you've done for me. I've never had friends like you. I'd take you over any of my own species if I had the choice."

"Then stay," Auphel said softly. Her own eyes were wet.

"I can't." I found Verelle's old book on the shelf. "I have to go, because this is what's got into my world. It's poison, isn't it? She's poison, even if she doesn't have her magic."

"Could you come back after she's dead?" Auphel asked. Zinian looked from her to me, eyebrows raised, a wild hope in his eyes that broke my heart.

"I'll try. I don't know anything about magic or how this works, but I will try. And if I can't, I'll never forget you." The lump in my throat choked off any more words, and when Auphel opened her arms, I got mine as far around her as I could and squeezed tight. "I love you, friend. Maybe that's a silly human thing to say, but I do."

"I'll remember you, too," she said, and released me. She thumped me affectionately on the shoulder, then sighed. "We should go. General Grys said I could come get you as long as we didn't take too long. I'd hate to make him mad at me again."

The streets were still quiet as we made our way to the palace. I drank everything in, from the cobblestone streets and pale grey walls of the buildings to the rich scents that rose from the bakery, run by a two-headed creature who made the most amazing treats when he got along with himself well enough to decide what to bake. A baby cried inside one of the little cottages that had once housed humans and were now home to the creatures whose labours had kept the human world alive and thriving for so many years.

The violence of my first days in the city had faded in my memory. I hoped that Auphel's keeping of the library would be a small step toward making sure that baby would never have to fight for her freedom. Maybe the monsters could keep from repeating the past, as humans seemed doomed to do forever. And maybe they could stay ready to protect themselves from another Verelle, should one ever arise.

Auphel led us to the dungeons. I shivered against the sudden chill in the air, but didn't step closer to her or Zinian for warmth. This was all business now. We'd had our goodbyes. It was time to let go.

Grys was waiting. So was Jaid, and the scholar Eriel. Jaid approached, tail curved into a question-mark shape behind one shoulder. It was the first time it hadn't lashed in irritation when she'd seen me. A small change, but a positive one. "Are you ready?"

"I think so," I lied.

She handed me the key, which felt heavier in my hand than I remembered. "Eriel will explain everything," Jaid said quietly. "I just wanted to say thank you."

I looked up into her citrine eyes. The slitted pupils were wide in the dark of the dungeon, giving her a sweeter look than I was accustomed to. "Um… you're welcome," I stammered.

"Are you glad to be going home?"

"No."

She nodded. "Duty, right? I understand that well." She shook my hand. "I'm almost sorry to see you go. You seem unlike the humans here, and… well, I may have misjudged you. Perhaps you staying wouldn't have been as terrible as I thought."

"Thank you. I think I'd have liked to have known you better." And it was true. Jaid had her scars just as Zinian had his, and they'd made her hate humans more vehemently than he did. But she could look past my physical form, as I could look past hers. I didn't think we'd ever have been friends, but we could have learned from each other.

Jaid stepped closer to Zinian and laid a hand on his shoulder. She leaned in close enough for her whiskers to tickle his face and whispered something to him. He winced, then nodded, and she let her hand fall.

Eriel took a shuffling step toward me. Her hooves made hollow clopping sounds on the stone floor.

"This is it," she said. "This door is imbued with new magic. All you need to do is unlock it and step through, and you'll be home. We don't know whether the doors work more than once, so try not to hesitate."

"I won't."

Grys snapped his fingers, and a group of twenty armed soldiers clattered around the corner. One carried Zinian's sword, another Auphel's axe. They would be ready for Verelle.

"We have soldiers waiting at the spot where she disappeared?" Zinian asked.

"We have. And a few other likely locations. We're ready."

Zinian's long fingers closed tight around the sword's grip, then relaxed into an easy and familiar hold. He looked at me, questioning. I nodded, and didn't try to say anything.

I wanted him to have his victory and his freedom as much as I wanted to see my world safe. He deserved that.

"Anything else?" I asked.

Eriel shook her heavy head. "I wish you well. May you find that everything in your world is as it should be, as we hope it will soon be in ours."

"Thanks."

My heart hammered as I stepped closer to the door. The key tingled in my hand.

I straightened my bag on my shoulder and felt the weight of the book and the tiny centaur-shaped pull-toy I'd decided at the last moment to take from my apartment.

I was too scared now to feel sad. At least that was something.

I slipped the key into the lock and turned it. The lock opened easily, almost eagerly, with a dull clunk that made my breath catch. I pulled the door open and held the key tight in my hand. If I was ever going to get back to Elurien, I'd need it.

Looking back hadn't been part of my plan, but I did. Auphel, Zinian, and Jaid stood together, ready to face the enemy they hoped would replace me. But the monsters' eyes weren't filled with rage and hate as they'd been the last time I'd seen them standing like this. Now it was sadness I saw there, and regret, and grim determination.

Zinian nodded gently. I turned to the door, gripped my bag tight, and stepped into the familiar darkness.

14

I fell longer and farther than I remembered falling before, and hit a hard surface with a thud. It cracked beneath me, and I slipped sideways. I'd had my eyes closed, but they snapped open as I scrambled to save myself. I grabbed onto a broken-off beam that stuck straight up beside my head.

The view was familiar, and yet not. The landscape of the island opened up around and below me, with no walls blocking the view. But there were no observation towers at this end of the island.

"Oh. Shit."

I was at the inn—or what was left of it. In fact, I seemed to have returned to the attic and then fallen another level down because there was no floor to support me. I was kneeling precariously on a cracked and tilted section of the boards that had run beneath the old carpets on the third floor. There was nothing around me. No staircase, no hall to follow. The upper levels of the inn, including the attic and the mysterious door, had been destroyed.

The town beyond didn't look like it was faring much better. Though landmark buildings still stood, several houses were in as rough shape as the inn was. I couldn't see more than that, but didn't have much hope that the damage was caused by some kind of freak storm.

No magic here, my ass. At least she was gone now. I just hoped I wouldn't have to answer questions about what had happened, and that Verelle was now being properly taken care of in Elurien. She deserved whatever she got.

I leaned out to see whether there were handholds I could use to get down to the second floor, and the beam I was holding snapped. I was too startled to scream as I plunged down, and barely had time to tuck my head close to my chest to try to protect myself before I hit the next floor hard. Bright and burning pain shot up from my right ankle, which had landed first and twisted beneath me.

I cried out at the pain and released a string of curses, then breathed deep to calm my nerves.

At least I'm down.

I reached for my bag, which lay a metre away on the filthy hallway carpet. There were few walls standing on this level, but at least the floor looked mostly solid. I'd be able to make my way to the staircase if I was careful.

I gasped. *The key.* It had been in my hand, but I didn't have it anymore, and couldn't see where I'd dropped it.

There. The key rested at the edge of a massive gap in the floor of what had been one of the inn's nicer bedrooms. Exposed pipes and wires stuck out from the hole.

I tried to stand, and my ankle buckled. I crawled toward the key.

The attic door was gone, but as long as I had the key, I had hope of returning. *There's always a door. The scholars said so.* My mouth went dry as I crept over the carpet, which was damp and slimy from exposure to the elements. I clenched my jaw and tested the floor ahead of me before each movement that took me closer to the key.

Please don't fall. I'm coming.

The floor shifted under me. I froze as I watched the key slip closer to the edge of the hole, then shrieked as the floor beneath my section of carpet crumbled and fell, clattering into a darkness that sounded like it went far deeper than the surface of the ground. My upper body was now supported only by a hammock of ancient carpet.

Shaking, I lay on my stomach and scooted closer until the tips of my fingers grazed the skull end of the key, which had miraculously stayed still. I gritted my teeth. *A little closer...*

I touched the key again and cried out as it slipped and tumbled into the black hole.

"No!"

I resisted the urge to dive after it.

I pushed myself to safety and then broke down, sobbing into my scratched-up hands. Maybe there had been no chance of going back. But if there had been, it was gone.

Pull yourself together, girl, my grandmother's voice admonished from deep in my memory, not unkindly.

I dragged myself to the stairwell and bumped my way down on my butt, as I would have when I was a little kid. I didn't fully trust the stairs, or my ankle. The office door at the bottom hung off its hinges and had been cracked down the middle. I went in, afraid of what I'd find, but the room was empty of people or bodies. I found a first aid kit in the desk and did a fair job of wrapping my sprained ankle tight in a tensor bandage. I was able to put some weight on it after that, though the pain persisted. I swallowed two expired ibuprofens dry and put the bottle into my bag.

My town needed me, and I now realized that maybe I needed them, too.

Gladys still rested in her place outside the inn, though the old Volkswagen had taken a few hits from falling debris that had dented her roof and hood. She looked like a foreign object, something from another world. I'd slipped behind the wheel before I remembered that I didn't have the keys, and that it was unlikely that anyone had fixed her in my absence.

"You're good for nothing, Gladys," I said aloud. "But it's nice to see you again."

I sat for a few moments to sort through my thoughts and formulate a plan. I needed a solid one now more than ever, but I needed information first. I'd limp into town, find out what had happened, make sure my parents were okay, then do what I could to help with rebuilding.

We had a lot of work to do before tourist season, thanks to Verelle.

I limped deeper into town, which showed no sign that as much time had passed here as had in Elurien. For all I could tell, I'd hardly been gone. Dust blew in tiny tornadoes through the asphalt play area of the school, and I paused. My stomach tightened as I felt something like the tingle I'd caught from the key.

Magic, lingering in our world.

They were wrong about her not having magic here. What if they were wrong about—

A dark speck appeared in the blue sky and flew closer until its wings stood clearly silhouetted. I scrambled under a picnic table and watched in horror as one of Verelle's angel-soldiers soared over, armed with a golden sword.

Where does one even get a golden sword around here? I wondered.

Not the point Hazel. Angel. Verelle's guards.

Verelle.

My breath became shallow, my thoughts jumbled. My chest tightened as though squeezed by giants' hands.

Not now. I squeezed my eyes closed, then opened them and forced myself to orient my senses, to recognize the feel of the ground beneath my hands, the damp smell of the ground, the bright green of the new blades of grass that pushed up from the dirt. Real things. Not speculation. Not fear.

The soldiers had lingered in Elurien long after Verelle was gone. Their presence here was a problem, but as long as she was gone and we could get some help from outside, we'd be okay. I wasn't going to panic. I'd just have to be more careful.

I waited until I was sure the soldier was gone, then limped to the ravine behind the school. At least the trees would provide some cover. I didn't meet any people hiding in the woods, but a black-and-white cat that lived at the used bookstore chased me down and wound between my legs, tripping me up. He'd never been particularly friendly when I'd worked there during high school. Times had changed.

"Hey, Tomie," I whispered. "What are you doing out?" That pampered beast had no street smarts. It was a wonder he hadn't died from lack of heated pillows and liver treats yet.

But of course he didn't answer in the way I could have reasonably expected in another world. He looked up and let out a loud "MEEERF!" before darting back into the bushes.

The ravine path led me to downtown Fairbrook, which no longer lived up to its name. I stuck to the shadows between the drugstore and the bookshop and took in the damage. It looked like a war zone. Cars lay flipped in the street with their windows smashed, and front rooms of stores had been gutted by fires now burned out.

"Oh, Hazel, what did you do?" I whispered. This was my fault. I hadn't meant to let a human monster into this world, but my hometown had suffered terribly for my curiosity. Maybe it was for the best that the key was gone. God knew what I might invite in if I tried to go back.

My unease grew as I made my way along the street, keeping my eyes open for signs of friends or enemies. The silence bothered me more than anything. Surely she hadn't killed everyone. These were humans. Her kind. Even if they lacked the "spark" of the people in her homeland, she'd have found them useful.

I hoped.

I found them in the town square. The square was the hub of the town in summer, swarming with tourists checking out the open-air craft market or enjoying the buskers who drifted in and out of town every summer. Even in the winter it was the social centre of the town, well maintained and well loved.

The pale spring grass on the green had been trampled flat, the high flower beds knocked over. The old-fashioned street-lamps were toppled like lumber. Burn marks marred the colourful siding of every building in sight, and in spite of the brightness of the day, a cloud seemed to hang over the square. The people of Fairbrook stood in a crowd facing the massive steps of the town hall, the only brick building in town. Their heads hung low, but their eyes were fixed on the top of the steps. Whatever had their attention was hidden from me, behind one of the ostentatious marble pillars outside the doors.

I moved closer, into the row of tall bushes in front of the building, creeping as silently as I could. At least the shrubs had been preserved, looking healthier than they should have been so early in the season. Thick leaves provided the perfect cover as I crawled through the dirt and dead foliage beneath, muddying my knees and my hands. When I reached the corner of the steps, I peered up onto the polished wooden porch.

She looked just like her doll. Tall and willowy, golden-haired and fair in every physical sense of the word. Verelle, alive and well and casting imperious glances over her new people as her soldiers paced behind the crowd, keeping them in line.

I fought the nausea that washed over me as I realized just how much deeper and more serious my problems had become.

15

I didn't dare move until the end of the meeting.

"Remember," Verelle announced. Her clear, sweet voice carried easily over the square. "I will treat you as well as you treat me." She waved her hand at the bushes, and they burst into pink blossoms that had no place on that particular species. I held in a sneeze as pollen exploded into the air. "I can restore your city, make it better than it's ever been. I bring such gifts for you!" She clasped her hands beneath her chin as though delighted by the idea.

"Wouldn't need improvement if she hadn't wrecked it," someone muttered in the front row. Jim Hancock, the pharmacist. I barely heard it, but Verelle had picked it up clearly. She shot him a disappointed look.

"Don't pout because I had to show my power before you would listen. I'll work wonders for you, and later for your whole world. I want your support so that I may bless you as I blessed the humans of my old home. They loved me, as you will. But my love does not come free. Go now, and make your decision."

She gathered the long skirts of a dress I suspected had been made of the mayor's office curtains and went inside. Several of her soldiers followed, while two remained outside the door, still as statues, swords drawn.

The people left, breaking into three groups: one group heading for the school, another moving toward the big white church on the hill, and the last ambling toward the nicer old houses near the square. Only the last group talked and laughed as they went.

I made my way back to the ravine, not wanting to cause a stir in public when people recognized me. Any surprise or excitement might be noted by the soldiers.

I'd have to be careful. Zinian had said that Verelle directed her soldiers' every movement. They'd lived without her when she'd disappeared, but had behaved like masterless puppets. With her here, they were capable of much more. I just didn't know exactly what.

I entered the convenience store by the broken back door. The place had been cleared out, but I found several fruit and nut bars that had fallen under a bottom shelf. I didn't look to see how long ago they might have been lost there. They tasted fine and they filled my stomach, and I didn't care about anything else.

I rested in the store room, and after sunset I made my way to the school. My ankle was bitching again, and I swallowed a few more pills on the way.

The school's outside doors were all locked, but I saw flickering light coming from the other side of the open gymnasium doors inside. I knocked as loud as I dared.

Three shadowed faces peered out of the gym, then came toward the door. They carried weapons, such as they were—a bright red fire extinguisher, an uncoupled fire hose held ready to be used as a whip, and the long wooden chalkboard pointer that old Mr. Goodyear had wielded during his fifty year reign at the school. They carried flashlights, which they promptly blinded me with.

"Who's there?" a familiar voice I couldn't place demanded.

"Hazel Walsh," I said, lowering the hand I'd thrown up to shield my face. The glass doors muffled our voices slightly, but weatherproofing for the school had never been high on the town's budget priorities.

"Hazel?" The one who had spoken stepped forward. Jimmy Wood, ruiner of reputations, knocker-up of cheerleaders, in the flesh. "How did you get here?"

"I drove."

Jimmy stepped back. "No one has been able to get onto or off the island for a week," he said.

So time had passed more slowly here than in Elurien.

"I drove in before that," I said. "I was at the inn when it collapsed." Not entirely true, but enough for now.

Jimmy's flashlight caught one of the other faces. Mrs. Perry, the vice principal. She squinted at me and shook her head. "Can't say. You know how that woman has tricked us."

The sound of wingbeats passed in the distance. I wasn't willing to be caught if he came closer. "Mrs. Perry, I went to this school when you started—" I did some mental math based on my grade "—ten years ago. I was here when Wiley Snow set the lab on fire. He was three years ahead of me. The smell lingered for weeks. I ate the soggy cabbage rolls every Tuesday that the church ladies cooked for us so the 'poor dears could have a real meal.' I graduated with honours. I came to help with my uncle's dairy bar."

The wings again, coming closer and then fading.

"Please," I added. "I'd stand out here and sing the school song for you, but I don't want to make more noise, and quite frankly I've forgotten the words because no one ever remembered to make us sing it."

Jimmy reached for the lock and let me in. I leapt into the school, and he caught me in one arm as he locked the door with the other.

The shadow of a winged soldier passed over the steps.

"Thank you," I sighed, and looked around. "Are there many people here? What the hell is happening?"

The third person, an older man I only knew by sight and not by name, brandished his floppy hose as threateningly as was possible. "I still have questions. If you arrived a week ago and survived the inn's collapse, where have you been?"

"Long story," I said. "I bet yours is more relevant."

He grunted and let me follow Jimmy toward the gym.

"It's good to see you, Hazel," Jimmy said. "How long has it been?"

"Years," I replied. "How's Jenny and the baby?"

"Oh. Can't say. They went to live with her aunt in Nova Scotia two years ago. Didn't work out after all."

Around fifty people occupied the gym, sitting on sleeping bags and cots. A handful of small children ran around, but most were adults, or nearly there. A good number of them were approaching half-past adult, with silver hair and wrinkled faces. I put as many names to faces as I could, orienting myself. This was my town, all right, if not the one I'd expected to find when I decided to come back. For a moment, I saw what mainlanders saw when they visited my hometown. *It's not so bad here, really. Even if—*

A scream echoed through the gym, and my mother clicked across the floor. I knew it was her before I saw her face. Only Loretta Walsh would wear high heels to the apocalypse.

She gripped my shoulders and pulled me into an unexpected hug. "You did come," she said. "You look horrible."

I resisted the urge to roll my eyes. "Thanks, Mom. You and Dad are okay?"

She sighed. "He's sleeping in the cafeteria. Fool broke his leg running from one of those angel things. Doc Saunders has him patched up and drugged up. You'll come see him when he wakes."

Not a question. Nothing ever was. I nodded and excused myself, and she went to sit with the church ladies.

It was good to know they were safe, or reasonably so. I just hoped they'd stay that way, and that I'd find a way to escape the suffocating feeling that was once again tightening like iron bands across my chest.

Welcome home, Hazel.

I sat with my back against the obnoxious primary-coloured wall beside the equipment locker and stretched my injured leg out in front of me. Jimmy ran around, gathering the people I supposed he considered important, and Mrs. Perry stood guard beside me.

"Tell me what's happening," I said. "I want to help."

She sighed. "Nobody knows what's happening. As I recall it, though, some of us awoke just over a week ago to the sound of the inn collapsing. Middle of the night. Volunteer crew went out to see what was happening and save Violetta James. Assuming she'd consent to being saved, of course."

I smiled to myself. I had sort of missed the familiarity of these people who knew each other so well. Big cities can't match that.

"She'd been crushed in her bed, which turned out to be a mercy for her. The boys dug through the rubble searching for whoever might have owned the car out front. Verelle emerged instead. Beautiful woman in a white dress, not a scratch on her. Wouldn't allow anyone to touch her, and—"

She hesitated.

"What?"

"Stories get muddled at that point. Simon Blackwood died. Some said he tripped. Some said she pushed him into the hole she'd rose from. A couple said he fell, but it was because she did something to him when he tried to touch her, like an electric shock that sent him flying. And that's how it's been since. She cut the island off. No traffic in or out, no electricity or phone, and the boats hit some kind of invisible wall half a kilometre out. The town's beat up, which was all her doing, and there are those angel things she keeps. There's a small faction thinks she really is from God as she claims, and she keeps them close and treats them well. Gave them the nice houses, and the stunned arses took them. The rest of us are confused. She's got some strange power like we've never seen. She's affecting our minds."

She looked at the man who'd stood with her in the foyer. "Samuel, has anyone seen Jim Hancock since he spoke up at the rally?"

It seemed strange to call such a dismal gathering a rally. Verelle's word, I was sure.

"No one," he said. "And you know, I keep forgetting to think of him."

"That's how it goes," Mrs. Perry told me. "Some of us remember better. Others could have seen him tortured in the street—and I wouldn't put it past that woman—and forget five minutes later that the man ever lived."

I shivered. I hadn't heard of anything like this when Zinian spoke about Verelle.

Jimmy had gathered a group of two dozen people and led them over. Mostly men, mostly middle-aged, all sober and solemn.

"You were in the inn when it collapsed?" asked Fred Blackwood, Simon's father and the other mechanic I might have consulted about Gladys.

"In a manner of speaking. I wasn't *there* there." I took a deep breath. They'd seen Verelle's magic. They'd have to believe me. "I went through a door into another world, one that was living in terror of Verelle. She somehow switched places with me. I came back in the hope that Verelle would be returned to that world."

No one spoke for a minute, until old David McMurtry clucked his tongue and shook his head. "The girl's got concussed," he said kindly. "Probably lost in the rubble of the inn, delirious and dehydrated, until she came and found us. God love her. Someone fetch a lemonade."

I accepted the lemonade, then shook my head. "I know it sounds ridiculous, but do you have a better explanation for her?"

Feet shuffled nervously in the small crowd. "Some thinks it's technological," Mr. McMurtry said. "Robots and such. Maybe drugs in the water supply. We're a little short on theories, and I'm sure we'll add yours to the list." He patted my head. "Tell me, were there fairies and monsters in this other world?"

"Yes," I grumbled, and ducked out from under his hand. "They're the ones the humans ruled over. There was a revolution."

Mrs. Perry sank to the floor beside me. "Hazel, my love. Was there a big talking lion wandering—"

"No. There was not."

"It doesn't matter," Jimmy said. "The fact is that however that Verelle got here, we're stuck with her until we do something."

It was easily the most sensible thing I'd ever heard Prettyboy McJockface say in all the time I'd known him. I nodded and finished my lemonade.

Jimmy motioned for the others to step closer. "Are we all ready?"

"For what?" I asked.

"Not you, gimpy," he said, not unkindly. We might have been friends if his teasing had been that gentle in school. "We're going after Verelle tonight. David still has his key for the town hall's back door."

I struggled to stand so I could talk sense to his face instead of his kneecaps. "Jimmy, you need a better plan than that. She'll be expecting it if she knows you all want her gone. She's lived through rebellions before, and she's well guarded."

"Don't worry," he said. "We've got a couple of shotguns, which if you're right about her origins, she hasn't dealt with before."

He almost sounded like he believed me.

"And if not," he continued. "We're splitting up to find the actual source of her so-called magic. It's got to be in that building. She almost never leaves."

I crossed my arms. "And what is it you think she's doing? How do you explain the soldiers?"

He frowned. "We don't explain them. We get rid of them."

My stomach sank. "You can't go in without knowing exactly what you're going to do and what you're facing. It's too big a risk."

Jimmy gave me a cocky smile. "No worries. We'll be back safe and sound with the island freed by morning."

They left, Mrs. Perry with them. I looked around the gym. Familiar faces, but no good friends of mine. I wondered whether the people I knew better were at the church, or if they'd been taken in by Verelle's speeches. It was hard to believe anyone would be.

She fooled Zinian, I reminded myself. And he was as smart as anyone I knew. But maybe that awareness had come later, after he saw the truth.

No one came closer to say hello. I supposed I must have been quite a sight with my tangled hair and weird clothes. A trip to the girls' bathroom confirmed all of that, and worse. My face was filthy and covered in scratches, as were my hands. I washed in a sink and did what I could with my hair, which I tied back with an abandoned pink elastic I found under the counter.

"Well, I'm not just going to sit here," I told my reflection. I would have, once. But I'd changed in the past few weeks. I'd survived a near-beheading, ventured into the desert with an ogre I called a friend, stood up to monsters, and won the heart of one of the best of them.

I'm different. I felt bigger than I had before. More capable. Braver. I didn't have a plan or a lucky charm, but I knew I might be able to help, and that was all I needed. I tightened the strap of my shoulder bag, asked Janet McMurtry to lock up after me, and headed out into the night.

The streets were quiet, as I'd expected. I stuck to the deepest shadows, hobbling as quickly as I could. I was rushing through an ink-black alley when I tripped over something soft and fell to my hands and knees.

"MEEEEEERF?"

"Tomie! Go home!"

The fat old cat rubbed against my face, and I wiped away the hairs that stuck to my sweaty skin. He followed when I started walking again, yelling the whole way.

"Dude, I don't have any tuna. Get lost."

I stepped out onto Main Street and ducked for cover as I caught sight of a pair of winged soldiers walking around the corner of a cross-street. One squinted in our direction, attention caught by the racket, and started coming our way.

I scooped Tomie up and carried him as quickly as I could out the far end of the alley. He purred and rubbed against my jaw until we reached the bookstore. The rear door stood open, and the store and the apartment above were empty. At least that was a relief. No bodies. But the Snows wouldn't have left Tomie to fend for himself. I wouldn't grieve yet, but I doubted they'd be back.

I fed the cat and left the open bag where he could reach it. He was obviously lonely, but I had somewhere to be, and I was already late.

I stroked a hand over the cat's fluffy coat. He ignored me as he chowed down on his kibble.

By the time I got to town hall, the lights were on inside. Someone was screaming.

"No," I whispered, and I ran in spite of the pain that shot up my ankle.

Shut up, you're not broken, I ordered. My ankle didn't comply, but I felt a little better.

I reached the sidewalk as the front doors burst open. A group of townspeople rushed out, prodded at swordpoint by a dozen soldiers. And then came Verelle, looking fresh and clean and perfect as though she hadn't been roused from sleep.

Maybe she hadn't. Maybe such a massive spark required no rest to keep burning.

I dove for the bushes.

"Is that all of them?" Verelle asked.

"We're still making our sweep," said a soldier, and I shivered at the sharp, crystalline tones of his voice. I hadn't realized her creations could talk. Or think.

"Finish it. I want all of them here."

She turned to the group. None dared to move with all of those swords pointed at them. Verelle motioned for a shotgun that one of the soldiers held, and she examined it carefully.

"You," she said. Jimmy looked up. "What is this? It killed one of my protectors."

He said nothing.

"Come here."

A soldier prodded Jimmy's back hard with his sword tip. Jimmy winced and stepped forward. Verelle handed him the gun.

"Shoot her," I whispered. But he was frozen, looking into her eyes.

"Show me how it works," she ordered. At the snap of her fingers, the soldiers brought Mrs. Perry onto the steps. "Kill her."

Jimmy blinked hard and shook his head. "I won't."

"I'll let you all go. If you don't, you die here."

Mrs. Perry's eyes grew wide. "Please," she said. "I have children. I'm educated, useful. Please."

Verelle smirked. "Come, young man. A demonstration, and you're free to play your little games and defy me another day. You came here to kill. Do it, and go."

She's enjoying this. It shouldn't have surprised me after what Zinian had told me, but seeing it was different. The sweat beading Jimmy's brow pleased her. Her eyes glowed as they took in the tremble in his hands. A musical laugh spilled from her lips as he raised the gun and lowered it.

Verelle's head tilted to one side, and her bright hair spilled over one shoulder, reflecting the moonlight. "She's going to die either way. I'm sure she'd like to die a hero."

Mrs. Perry whimpered.

I took a mental count of the townspeople. There had been more, I was sure of it.

Jimmy continued to hesitate. "This isn't how it's done," he said.

"No?" Verelle sounded genuinely interested, but I caught a hint of amusement. "So breaking in to assassinate good folk is fine, but making criminals pay for their crimes isn't? I'm afraid your world befuddles me terribly. Kill her now."

Jimmy raised the gun and pointed it at Mrs. Perry.

Then he turned, quick as a lightning strike, toward Verelle.

She was ready for him. She raised a hand as he pulled the trigger. The gun went off with a deafening roar, but it was Jimmy who fell, soaking the concrete with his blood. I choked back a scream. Another flick of Verelle's fingers, and the others all fell to the ground, writhing, bleeding from their mouths and eyes.

Her eyes flashed as she turned to the brick building behind her. Another shot rang out from a window, and she deflected another bullet.

"Six more in the building," she said. "Five men and another woman. Finish them quickly. These people bore me. No mind for games, any of them."

She swept into the town hall, skirts trailing behind her.

My entire body trembled, and my breath came in gasps when I remembered to take them. I sat in the shelter of the bushes with my head between my knees until my heart stopped pounding and the silent, panicked tears that wetted my cheeks slowed.

Rushing over there wouldn't help the people at the bottom of the steps. They already lay still, every one of them, and I had no desire to find out exactly what she'd done.

I couldn't make sense of anything, and I couldn't go back and face the people at the school. Not yet. I needed room to think.

Tomie greeted me with a soft mew when I dragged myself into the apartment above the bookshop.

I dropped my bag to the floor and crawled into the double bed in the corner. But comfortable as it was, and reassuring as Tomie's purrs were when he curled up at my feet, my racing thoughts wouldn't let me sleep.

What happened?

Well, they'd gone in not knowing what they were facing.

So what more do I know now?

She could kill with magic. That wasn't a surprise. And she kept people alive as long as they interested her. Something I'd known, but understood better now.

How did she know about the other people? She hadn't just known where they were. She'd known everything but their names—and maybe she knew those, but didn't care.

She must have sensed them in the building somehow... But then why didn't she know I was there? I'd been right beside the steps, watching everything, terrified and trying not to scream.

I rolled over, and a disgruntled cat crept up to sleep on the pillow above my head.

Jimmy had known who was missing. She'd known to prepare for an attack from behind because he knew it was coming. She was ready when he turned the gun on her, because she knew he was going to do it. But he hadn't known about me, so neither had she.

She'd read his mind.

I shuddered and curled into a ball.

I need my friends. I need advice. I need… I sighed. I just needed them period. Especially Zinian. He'd help me think of a plan. Obviously Verelle's powers were different here, but we'd come up with something together.

I sat up and went to get more pills for my throbbing ankle. As I picked up my bag, Verelle's old book slipped to the floor.

If I couldn't sleep, I could study the enemy. The copy of the Verhumn in the library had told stories about Verelle at the back. I'd read all night if it could give me some insight.

I searched the kitchen cupboards by the moonlight that shone through the window and found a trio of candles and a few matches. I stayed well away from the windows to hide the light that might give me away. Curled up in a big armchair with a glass of water on the table beside me, I flipped to the back of the book.

And found nothing about Verelle.

I looked more closely. No pages were missing, but this version ended far earlier than the one in the library. A sense of cool calm settled over me as I realized that the book I held was older than I'd realized.

Older than Verelle, or at least close to it.

Old enough that she hadn't influenced human beliefs and history yet.

I sipped my water and flipped to the beginning again. Hadn't I thought that what I read in the library seemed off?

There.

And in those days the monsters roamed the land, living as animals, without understanding. The humans came among them, living in peace, sharing the words of the Mother.

The later version had spoken of the humans' duty to subdue the beasts and rule over them. A small change in the words, and worlds of difference in meaning.

I rubbed the thin, powdery paper between my fingers as I wondered how she'd done it. Verelle had gained power through her magic, no question. But the people hadn't seen her just as a queen or a leader. She'd been the closest thing they had to an earthly god. Generations had been raised believing what she wanted them to believe, because she'd been around early enough to influence the words they believed to be divinely inspired.

Her power had been absolute, because who would defy the will of the Mother? And Verelle had made sure she was their goddess' beloved mouthpiece.

I dove into the old book. It looked fairly standard, from what I knew about religious texts. Little about monsters after that first entry, other than metaphorical mentions. Perhaps the original author had considered that subject closed. I did find admonitions against killing, praise for peaceful behaviours, and warnings that deeds returned to their doers tenfold.

I wondered how heavily Verelle had managed to edit all of those commandments.

Sleep finally caught up with me. My mind became fuzzy, my eyelids heavy. I curled up with the old book clutched in my hands and let myself drift off.

My last thought as sleep overcame me was that I wished I had more help, but even without it, I'd see that Verelle paid for her deceit and her crimes. If Zinian couldn't be here to finish his work, I'd do it for him.

Somehow.

16

A week passed, and our world grew smaller.

The people who had been sheltering at the church moved down to the school when they heard about that group's loss, and I joined them rather than keeping my cozy shelter above the bookstore. I'd spent years trying to escape these people, but we'd all be better off if we stuck together now. We spread out from the gym and set up camp in the classrooms, packed in tight, making the best of it.

Anything we needed from outside came at a steep price. A run to the hardware store netted us sleeping bags and camp stoves, but cost us several people who were hauled away by the soldiers, screaming. We cleaned out McMurtry's Grocery after the school cafeteria's supplies ran out, a successful mission carried out under the cover of night. But McMurtry's was a small store. The food we scraped together didn't last long, and the only other grocery store was too far to risk the journey.

Even if we got there, Verelle would starve us out eventually. She seemed content to leave us to our sad little fortress, only terrorizing those who dared leave in search of the supplies that kept us alive. But we would end up submitting to her out of need or dying in our defiance.

I didn't like to think of what might be happening to the people who had already been taken.

We lost people almost every night, though not to the soldiers. They never said goodbye, but slipped out and went to join Verelle's faithful. I wondered what it cost them to be warm and fed.

As for me, I gave my report on the town hall incident, then rested and let my leg heal. Once I was back on my feet I helped with the children, who were having a hard time dealing with the strange situation. I told them stories about friendly monsters when the school's shadows frightened them, and silly tales about dragons slaying arrogant magical knights who spoke a lot like Verelle.

At least the children accepted stories about monsters. In spite of the undeniable evidence of Verelle's unearthly powers, the adults in town clearly thought I was crazy when I tried to talk about how the monsters had overthrown her in another world. I learned to keep quiet, but their disbelief grated on me.

It was a Tuesday evening—or I guessed it was, I'd lost track without my planner—when my turn came to help with a supply run. Gus Hodder, the owner of the larger grocery store, had made a brave journey home to get his van. Though we knew the noise would draw the soldiers' attention, the people heading out were well armed and thought it worth the risk. Visions of non-perishable food items danced in everyone's heads, mine included, and I felt healed enough to go.

Six of us piled into the back of the white van—enough to load it, but not so many that we wouldn't have room to pack the thing with food, medicine, and whatever else we found. We didn't speak as the van bumped over freshly potholed roads. The soft purr of its engine seemed loud enough to wake those who had already died, and certainly enough to catch a sentry's attention, but we made it to the Sav-Mor without encountering a single soldier.

We hustled out and entered through the door beside the loading bay. Without overhead lights, the storage room was a black maze of boxes and plastic-wrapped pallets where anything might be lurking. There was a time when I might have been afraid of hidden monsters. Now, I couldn't think of anything that would be more welcome. Even a ghost or two wouldn't have bothered me.

There were worse things outside.

We did our work quickly, following silent orders, taking what our mission leader pointed out with the beam of his flashlight. Soon enough we were back in the van. I sat in the front with Gus and a skinny kid named Stan.

"That was too easy," someone muttered, and my heart skipped a beat.

I hadn't left all of my superstitions behind.

A block later, something slammed into us from outside. The vehicle rocked to one side. Gus hit the gas, any hope of getting to the school unnoticed forgotten, and the van roared toward safety.

We were almost there when a second hit came, harder. The next few seconds passed in a rush that seemed to last forever as the van tipped, flipped, and slid on its side. Someone cried out in the back, barely audible over the crashing of boxes and clang of cans.

We came to a stop. Silence followed.

"We have to get out of here," someone groaned.

"No," I said, and shifted against the tight seatbelt that kept me from breathing properly. "They're out there, waiting for us."

"So we stay here forever?"

I had no answer for that. We were screwed either way, and whoever was out there knew it.

Those of us in the front seats released our seatbelts and arranged ourselves so we weren't stepping on each other too much. Those in the back managed as well as they could in the mess. Tim Nippard had a broken arm, and Sadie Mercer had been knocked out. They needed to get to the school. Sadie's kids would be waiting.

I pressed my face to the dirty windshield. The moon wasn't as bright as it had been weeks before, but I made out the shapes of two soldiers pacing around, waiting for us. I took a deep breath.

"I'm going to distract them," I said. "Someone else needs to come. We'll split up, take them in different directions. The rest of you can carry Sadie to the school. Who's coming?"

"Guess that'll be me." Gus handed the store and van keys to Stan. "Hope to see you all at the school, but just in case." He pushed my door open, and we climbed out.

The soldiers gave us time to hit the ground running. *Decent of them*, I thought, and wondered whether they shared Verelle's love of cruel games or were just following orders. Gus took off down the street, away from the school, one soldier behind him. I dashed for the park.

No footsteps behind me. I ran into an alley, where wings would be useless, and stopped to see if my soldier was going to try to cut me off. A trash can hit the ground behind me, and I continued forward. Beyond the end of the alley, the thick trees of the park beckoned, promising at least the illusion of safety. If I could make it to the creek and into a drainage culvert, I might lose him.

If.

I ran. The sneakers I'd found in a school locker slapped the ground, echoing like gunshots. Thirty paces to the woods. Twenty. Ten.

My ankle went out from under me as a familiar sharp pain shot up my leg.

I cried out in surprise as much as pain as I hit the ground. Gravel tore into my palms and ground into the knees of my pants. I turned to see eight winged soldiers approaching slowly, swords drawn.

I didn't know which had started the pursuit, so I spoke to all of them.

"Had to call in reinforcements to deal with one little girl?"

Their blank, beautiful faces didn't register understanding or irritation. They stepped closer, circling around me.

I tried to stand, and my ankle buckled again. One of the soldiers raised his sword.

Heavy footsteps approached, accompanied by a roar that shook my bones. I gasped and curled into a ball on the ground, making myself as small as possible as the clash of weapons rang out above me.

Someone kicked me, and I looked up long enough to see that the way to the park was clear. I dragged myself to the edge of the trees and turned back. The scene was chaotic and the street dark, but I would have recognized my rescuers anywhere.

Auphel stood with a soldier pinned under her foot. She brought her axe down, cleaving his torso neatly in half, and swung at another who ran at her from the side. His sword caught her arm as he ducked under the axe, and she roared in pain. A moment later his throat was in her hand, and his neck snapped. Zinian and Jaid each took down two soldiers with swords and claws, then turned to finish the others. One took off into the air, and Zinian followed. The feathered body hit the ground with a sick thud a moment later, gutted and bleeding.

Zinian landed, and all three turned to me. Jaid's wide eyes took in the buildings that faced the park as she caught her breath. Her tail swished madly, and her hair stood on end. "Are there more?"

I stood and leaned my weight on my good ankle. "More around. I think that's all for that bunch. Where… How…" I stopped to take a breath, and let out a short, shocked laugh. "It's really good to see you guys."

My heart swelled as I drank in the glorious sight of monsters in Fairbrook. I hadn't let myself fully understand how much I'd missed them until I had them back. My dear Auphel. The fearsome and loyal Jaid, on my side at last. And Zinian... *God.* Had I really thought I could keep myself from falling for this strange, beautiful person?

Zinian looked me over, taking in my obvious injury. He didn't smile, but his relief was clear in his eyes. "The where and the how can wait. Verelle might not know exactly what happened, but she'll know someone killed her soldiers. Where can we go and be hidden?"

"We're all taking shelter at the school. It's a few blocks away, though. Auphel, are you okay?"

The ogress nodded, but held her arm out. Blood flowed freely from her wound. "I should wrap this so I don't leave a trail."

Jaid removed her sash and bandaged Auphel's arm. The ogress winced as Jaid pulled it tight, but didn't complain.

"Better to get away from here," Jaid said, and nudged a body with her foot. "I'm guessing by the fact that they're not disappearing that Verelle is here and alive?"

"Very much so," I said. I explained what I understood of the situation as we walked, speaking quietly. Zinian's arm around my waist and his body pressed against mine felt so good that they almost made it worth getting attacked and almost killed.

Again.

"But how did you get here?" I asked.

Jaid clucked her tongue. "Zinian nearly lost his mind when you disappeared and Verelle didn't come back. Grys believed that Verelle was either dead or had reappeared somewhere else."

"But you disagreed?" I asked Zinian.

"I didn't know. That was the problem. I wasn't willing to let it go until we were sure she wasn't here with you. Verelle is clever, and knows how to control magic. I thought she might have found a way to stay if she wanted to."

"Guess you were right," Auphel said glumly.

"But I had the key," I said. "Until I lost it."

Jaid's whiskers twitched. "It turns out that the spark is a myth, as many of us suspected. We haven't found a monster who's gifted with magic as Verelle is, but then, not many humans were, either. Creating another key was a matter of finding the right information, equipment, and materials. It's not the same as yours, but it worked."

"It took far too much time, though," Zinian added. "I didn't think we'd find you alive."

"I was going to comment on your impressive timing," I said, "but I think it moves more slowly here."

"Oh, good," Auphel said. "Maybe we'll get back before Grys notices we're gone."

I smiled at her. "I appreciate you all coming."

Jaid grunted. "I couldn't let Zinian pursue his obsessions without me. And when Auphel found out, there was no stopping her."

"I don't like this place," Auphel whispered. She knocked into a pile of crates and scrambled to catch them before they toppled. "It smells funny."

We approached the rear doors of the school. I didn't want to cause panic in the school, but felt certain that we needed all the help we could get. Between my friends and the townspeople, we could handle Verelle.

I couldn't wait to show them all how entirely not-crazy I was.

The others hung back as I knocked. Mr. Hicks from the tourism hut opened the door.

"Did the others make it?" I asked.

"All but Gus. He's not with you?"

"No. But I found some help." I hesitated for a moment. "Bring a few of the leaders. No one who's easily spooked. I have a secret weapon, but we'll want to keep it quiet for now." I wouldn't force my friends to sleep in the school, but an introduction or two would warm people to the idea of our odd saviours and allow the townspeople to help plan our attack.

Mr. Hicks gave me a suspicious look, but let me take the door and headed off toward the teachers' lounge. I motioned for my friends to come in.

"It smells worse in here," Auphel grumbled. "Like humans, but dirtier."

She sat on the stairway beside the door and picked at her bandage.

"How will they react to us?" Zinian asked. "I don't expect we—"

A scream interrupted him.

"Maybe not so good," I admitted.

The scream had come from Mr. Hicks. He'd brought a dozen people with him—not all leaders, but likely all curious. A woman grabbed the child who had accompanied her and sprinted off down the hall. My mother stood with a pale face, trembling.

Perfect.

"It's fine!" I yelled. "These are the monsters I told you about. They're here to help us!"

Someone sobbed at the back of the crowd. Auphel stepped deeper into the shadows.

I gritted my teeth and reminded myself that I'd been scared at first, too. "Listen to me. You have nothing to be afraid of."

"This is the end times," an old woman moaned. One of the church ladies who had been friends with my gran, but I couldn't remember her name now. "Angels and devils and monsters!" Her fingers scrabbled at her throat as though searching for pearls to clutch.

"Shut up," I ordered. She gasped. "You're all acting like these guys are worse than the ones who are trying to kill us. They've taken Verelle down before, and now they're willing to help us. Are you going to let them come in?"

No one moved.

"You see, Hazel," Mr. Hicks said, having regained a little of his composure, "we don't know them. And maybe they're helpful as you say, but we have the children to think of. And we don't want to draw more attention. We'll have to talk it over."

I glanced at Jaid, who rolled her eyes. I couldn't have agreed more.

"Fine," I said. "It's probably better if you just let us handle it. Verelle will be gone before you know it, and you can start rebuilding before the tourists descend. But I need you to promise that you'll stay put. No one leaves the building for any reason until we come to get you. Clear?"

Mr. Hicks nodded.

"Just a moment," my mother said, having found her voice at last. I'd never seen her speechless for so long. "Hazel Anne Walsh, you will come back to the gymnasium right now." I was touched by her concern for my safety until she added, "No daughter of mine is going to go gallivanting about with demons and monsters and God knows what else."

"Mom."

She didn't hear me. She was working up to a proper rant. "Your grandmother must be rolling in her grave. What did you get mixed up with when you went away, young lady? I can only imagine what Pastor Tulk would say about—"

"MOM," I bellowed, and she stopped.

"Hazel Anne—"

"Loretta Jean. Please fuck off."

Her lips disappeared in a tight line, and she stalked away. I felt bad. But only a little. I'd wanted to say that for the past decade, and it had been even more satisfying than I'd expected.

"We're going to take care of this." I made eye contact with everyone to make sure they were listening, and one by one they nodded.

"She can see your thoughts," I added. "I know a lot of you didn't believe me when I talked about magic, but my friends here are proof that I'm not crazy. I don't want Verelle knowing about these secret weapons. So don't move. Bar the doors until tomorrow night."

I turned on my heel and left in as dignified a manner as I could with most of my weight on one foot. Auphel scooped me up under her good arm, erasing the last of my dignity but preserving some of my energy.

"Where to?" she asked, and I pointed toward the bookstore.

Tomie greeted me with a loud mew, then hissed at my guests and ran to hide behind a stack of thrillers. "Don't take it personally," I told them. "In this world, you're terrifying."

Jaid sniffed. "I'm terrifying in mine, too. How quickly you forget."

Zinian smiled at his friend.

Auphel wasn't going to fit up the narrow staircase to the apartment, so we stayed among the stacks of dusty books on the ground floor. Tomie showed his face again after a few minutes and planted himself on Jaid's lap, purring. The felid woman scratched his back gently with her claws.

I sat in an armchair, and Zinian sat on the floor next to my legs with one hand wrapped gently around my injured ankle. I drank in the sight of him, though I could barely see him in the gloom of the shop. He leaned toward me as I ran my fingers through his hair.

"I can see everything you're doing," Jaid noted. "Fair warning."

At least she seemed used to the idea of us. That was something.

I explained what had happened the night the people attacked the town hall, and the conclusions I'd drawn.

"I can't disagree," Zinian said, "though it troubles me that she has different powers here. This would be easier if we knew exactly what we were dealing with."

"What's the plan, then?" Jaid asked.

We sat in silence, thinking. The sky outside the windows began to lighten in spite of the grey clouds that had gathered in the past few hours.

"We can't have a plan," I said, almost to myself. They all looked at me. "If we have a plan, she'll know it as soon as she looks at us. There's no element of surprise with her now."

"And we don't have the forces for an open attack this time," Zinian added. "We could just try to sneak up, but she'll be alert."

"We need someone with no knowledge of any plan to distract Verelle," Jaid said. She scratched under her chin. "Someone who can hold her attention. It'll make the rest of our jobs easier, and her soldiers get sluggish when she's not focused on them. I would offer to do it, but—"

"But we want to keep you three a secret," I finished for her. "The less she realizes about the comings and goings between our worlds, the better. It has to be someone from town. Someone who will try not to think about the fact that monsters have arrived, even though I'm sure everyone has heard by now." I swallowed hard. "Someone who cares enough to want to keep you safe."

Zinian's hand tightened around my ankle, and I winced.

The idea of leaping without looking, of walking up to Verelle with a head full of nothing and trying to keep her distracted terrified me. I liked plans. I needed control. Anything else was a recipe for disaster. And yet there was nothing else for it.

I leaned over and rested my cheek against one of Zinian's horns. "I'll get out of your way while you make your plans. Make them good. I'll figure out my distraction."

"For when?" Auphel asked.

"She holds outdoor meetings for her faithful every morning," I said. "Assuming the rain holds off, that would be a good time. She'll be exposed then."

I went up to the apartment and rewrapped my ankle, grabbed a granola bar and a bottle of water, then slipped the ancient, untitled copy of the *Verhumn* into my bag. Zinian met me near the top of the stairs as I started down. His wings filled the space behind him, preventing escape.

As if I'd want to.

I wrapped my arms around his neck and buried my face against him. We stood like that for several minutes, not speaking, bodies pressed together.

"I can't believe you came for me," I murmured.

"I had no choice," he said, and pulled his claws through my tangled hair. "I thought I was going to go insane with worry." He kissed me, long and deep, and for a brief moment I forgot everything else. "I should never have let you come back."

"I guess it was a good thing for Fairbrook that I did."

"I don't care about Fairbrook. I care about you." He pressed his forehead to mine and looked into my eyes. "Be careful, Hazel. I promise we'll do everything we can to finish her before she hurts you." His thick brows gathered into a concerned frown. "You know what you want to do?"

"I have an idea."

An idea, but not a plan.

It would have to be enough.

17

*D*eep breaths.

I considered the mental exercises that were supposed to help when I felt anxious. I didn't want to close my eyes and picture serene surroundings, but I tried to clear my mind and ground myself in the quiet of the park as I sat hidden in the bushes, waiting for the appointed time.

And I tried to ignore the eerie lack of bird sounds that I'd been too distracted to notice before.

I watched a pair of soldiers soar over the pond and wondered whether the loss of so many yesterday had affected them. They'd be on high alert, surely. I hoped Verelle was going mad as she tried to figure out how the stubborn people of the school had killed her warriors.

I hoped she was terrified.

I paged though Verelle's book, deciding that it would be my focus. I let my indignation and anger grow, followed my thoughts down rabbit holes of what might have been if not for her. The book in my hands may or may not have been divinely inspired, but it seemed a fine blueprint for a peaceful world. Of course, people would have found a way to reinterpret it to fit their own views and desires, picking and choosing passages and probably ignoring the larger message. But it would have had a chance to do good, and that was what pissed me off. I didn't know how she'd managed it, but Verelle had rewritten a religion to suit her, warped it to create a world of oppression, inequality, and chaos. She'd used it to hurt people I loved dearly.

I'd never cared for anger. It seemed pointless, and became frightening when it got out of control. But just this once, I let it take me. Hot tears slipped down my cheeks as I thought of the deaths she'd caused, of the humans who might have been good if they'd believed they served a kind and loving Mother or been free to choose for themselves. Or maybe they would still have been assholes. Thanks to Verelle, we'd never know.

I started for the town hall building. Verelle's faithful would be gathering now. I had to keep my eyes on the sidewalk, but kept looking back to the pages.

Focus. This is all there is.

No thoughts of Zinian and the others, no fear that they wouldn't come up with a plan that would end her and save me. Only my anger, and the desire to reveal to the town what she really was.

The townspeople had set up folding chairs below the steps in spite of the threat of rain: two sections in neat rows with a wide aisle in the middle, like a church. I'd heard about it from the others, how she stood and spoke to her faithful, how they stared adoringly. Actually seeing it nauseated me. Verelle stood in a flowing white gown not unlike the one I'd worn to my first supper with Zinian. She looked positively angelic, but it was the two soldiers standing at the bottom of the steps who bore the wings. I hung back at the edge of the square and watched. No more soldiers flew overhead. The others would be out patrolling.

Verelle knew her own strength well enough that she felt confident sending them elsewhere. I just hoped I wasn't wrong about her weaknesses.

Don't think about weaknesses. This isn't a plan. Just be angry.

I opened the book, not realizing how tightly I was gripping the pages until one pulled free of the ancient binding and fluttered away on a gust of wind.

Verelle saw me coming, but kept speaking to her people. A low chuckle rippled through the crowd, but I was still too far away to hear what she'd said.

As I reached the last row of chairs, I began to read aloud. Quietly at first, then growing louder as my anger gave me confidence. A poem from the middle, in which the centaur was a metaphor for the unity of man and beast. I didn't remember seeing that in the newer version at all.

Verelle stopped speaking and watched me, her mouth twisted into a tight smile.

At least I have her attention. I paged back.

"*'And in those days the monsters roamed the land,'*" I read, voice only trembling slightly. Everyone turned to watch as I approached and stopped several paces from the bottom step. *"'Living as animals, without understanding. The humans came among them, living in peace, sharing the words of the Mother.'"* I looked up at her and met her eyes. "What peace did you bring to the last world you nearly destroyed, Verelle?"

Even up close, it was hard to read her expression. She appeared interested, even somewhat amused, but irritated. Trying, I suspected, to decide whether to make an example of me right away or let me dig my own grave a little deeper.

"Where did you get that, child?"

I wanted to turn to address the people, but I needed her full attention. I refused to look into her eyes even as I felt her in my thoughts, observing them. I hoped my anger burned her.

"I visited Elurien," I told her. "I arrived as you left."

One finely shaped eyebrow arched. "Was that you? I owe you thanks for opening the door." She raised her arms. "All of my people owe you thanks!"

A few applauded uncertainly behind me.

"This isn't the message that the people were reading when I was there," I said, and pointed the book at her. "How old are you, Verelle? How many generations did it take you to reshape these words and the beliefs that came from them?" I stepped closer. "Was it hard to convince the priests to omit the message of peace and include one of cruelty? Or did it only take a display of your so-called divine power?"

She shrugged. Apparently bad-guy blabbermouth wasn't her thing. Too bad for me.

"The spark is bullshit," I continued, "but you made them believe. It's most impressive."

Verelle chuckled. "We all carry the spark. Every human here before me. Even you."

A dark shape flew up to the roof of the building behind her. I didn't let myself consciously note it.

A thought struck me. "Do you ever laugh at the perfect absurdity of it all?"

She frowned.

"You're so concerned with humans, with convincing them that they're the rulers of your world... but look at you. What you call a divine spark is really an accident of birth, isn't it? Your magic is impressive, no doubt. But no goddess who intended people to live by this—" I shook the book at her" — would ever purposely give such power to someone who would use it as you have. You're an inhuman oddity just as much as the monsters you hate so much."

Her eyes flashed, and she bared her teeth. "How dare you? I am the pinnacle of what is human. I am eternal, undying, blessed."

"As no natural human is," I concluded for her. "Yet you used your power for your own selfish purposes, to gain power and create slaves." For the benefit of the audience sitting silent behind me, I added, "You tortured innocent creatures for the sake of your own sick pleasure. Is that why your dear Mother blessed you? To bring suffering to her world?"

"Liar," Verelle spat.

Murmurs spread through the crowd behind me as I flipped to a passage I'd once misunderstood.

"'*Beware the liar,*'" I read, louder now. "'*The disrupter, who seems to come in peace. Beware the true monster, fair of face and black of heart, with words of honey and claws of poison.*' That's you, isn't it? When the Mother of your world first whispered words into the ears of humans, she warned them about you. Was this the first passage you had removed?"

Verelle's pale cheeks reddened. She raised a hand. A familiar feline form prowled onto the steps behind her, but again I ignored it. And so did the soldiers, who were as focused on me as Verelle was.

"Go ahead," I yelled, and spread my arms wide. "Shut me up. Show them how afraid you are of the truth coming out. Did you think you could have a fresh start here?"

Verelle wasn't so pretty when rage gripped her. She screamed and lowered her hand. At the same time, a massive shape flew at me from my right and hit me hard, sending me crashing to the ground several metres away. My head hit the concrete sidewalk, sending shooting stars across my vision, but I pushed myself to my feet and stumbled to the bottom of the steps, where Auphel was slumped in a motionless heap, struck by whatever the sorceress had intended for me. Her battle axe lay useless at Verelle's feet.

I stumbled to Auphel and rolled her onto her back. She was breathing but unconscious, eyes staring up into the clouds.

I glared up at Verelle, who stood unharmed, shock painted plainly across her face.

The soldiers roused themselves then, as Verelle realized she was under attack. Jaid leapt at one and tore his throat out, leaving him bleeding as she met the other blade to blade.

Verelle looked to the sky as though to call for her other warriors, and found a very different winged shape descending, sword drawn.

She gasped, and the anger left her face as he landed. "My angel. You've returned to me."

Something caught in her voice then. I hated to think it was sadness. She had no right to feel that. Or regret. She was only allowed to be the bad guy, and I was happier without any shades of grey there.

"It's over, Verelle," Zinian said. "You put up a worthy fight, but for far too long."

"Zinian," she said, with nauseating tenderness. "I tried to make you happy."

He snarled. "You failed."

"Yet I heard so few complaints, my darling."

She reached out a hand and wiggled her fingers, and Auphel's back arched in a spasm. She groaned. With a flick of Verelle's wrist, I felt it too. I gasped as electric pain radiated from my heart to the tips of my limbs, and my jaw clenched tight. I couldn't speak. Couldn't breathe.

Zinian bared his teeth and drew his sword. Verelle laughed and turned the blade aside with her magic, as though pushing away a child's toy.

"You were always so endearingly noble about monsters," she said. Auphel groaned as another spasm gripped her. Verelle's expression grew cold. "Toss your sword aside, or these friends of yours die."

Zinian looked at us, hesitating, then growled in frustration. His sword clattered to the boards and slid off into the bushes.

No. I fought to stay conscious, to draw a breath and yell for him to attack.

Auphel lay still as Verelle's attention turned completely on Zinian. My own pain disappeared, leaving me trembling, but intact. Verelle had found a more interesting playmate. I tried to get to my feet, but my legs collapsed under me.

"That's better," Verelle said to him, and smiled. "What a mess this has become. I trusted you, my angel. It broke my heart when you betrayed me, and an ancient heart is not an easy thing to harm. But now you're here, which means you've found a way home. Come home with me. It will be different this time."

She tilted her head again, an innocent gesture I was already getting sick of.

Behind them, Jaid took a blade to the arm and screamed in rage. Zinian didn't look, and I wondered whether Verelle might be soothing his emotions, making him forget us as she'd made the people of Fairbrook forget those who had been lost.

Auphel stirred, and I looked down at her. "Shhhh," she whispered.

My throat tightened.

"Step aside now," the ogress said softly.

I pushed away, heart in my throat. Auphel hauled herself up to a crouch and bellowed, then stumbled up the steps, wobbling drunkenly. Verelle turned and blasted her again, leaning forward with the force of her magic. Auphel fell, crashing head first to the ground with a sickening thud.

"Auphel!" I cried.

In that moment when Verelle's attention was diverted, Zinian lunged for Auphel's axe. Though I would have guessed that no one short of an ogre could lift it, he grabbed the handle and swung it in a massive arc. Verelle saw it coming, but momentum brought it down hard and heavy in spite of her magic.

Time seemed to slow to near-freezing as the blade came down on the back of Verelle's neck. I half expected it to bounce off, but it sliced clean through and slammed into the wooden boards below, shattering them.

Verelle's golden hair flew as her head rolled and bounced down the steps, coming to a stop near my feet. She looked up at me, blinking, looking quite bewildered. Her lips twitched, trying to form words and not finding the breath to make herself heard.

Auphel took a sharp breath as her eyes snapped open. My heart leapt.

"Here," Auphel croaked. I grabbed the head by its hair and tossed it to her. Golden hairs tangled in my fingers, and I fought back my gag reflex. Auphel twisted toward it and brought one fist down, crushing Verelle's skull.

Everything Verelle had ever been—every hate, every lust, every bit of wasted potential—turned to pale, bloody mush.

I caught my breath as I crouched beside Auphel. She was having trouble breathing, and blood flowed like tears from her eyes. I touched her hand, and her fingers curled around mine, enveloping them in her grasp.

Jaid set her sword down and leaned against a wall to catch her breath. Her enemy had disappeared. I hoped all of the others had, as well.

Zinian stumbled down the steps and placed a hand on Auphel's face. "You in there, soldier?"

"I'm here," she croaked. "I'd like to sleep for a month, if that's okay."

Zinian let out a relieved breath. "Maybe after we get you home. Heroes deserve all the rest they want." He patted her shoulder, then stretched his arms out and winced. "That's going to hurt later. How do you manage to carry that axe everywhere with you?"

Auphel smiled and let out a barking cough that made me stumble away. "Guess I'm as useful as you always said I was."

I looked around. Everyone had fled, likely when the monsters appeared. I hoped some had stayed long enough to see how they'd saved us.

Jaid's fur bristled with excitement as she came toward us.

"It worked," she said. "You okay, Zin?"

Zinian nodded. The dark circles under his eyes and the bend of his neck revealed his deep exhaustion, but he smiled, then laughed. "It's over."

Jaid stepped closer and waited, tail twitching, until I looked up at her. "You did well," she said. "For a human and a civilian. Thank you for not giving us away."

I smiled a little, though the shock of everything that had just happened made it feel false. "Not for all of Verelle's power would I have given you up."

She wrinkled her nose, lifting whiskers that were now bent and broken. "I hope you wouldn't want that."

I snorted. "Not even a little."

Jaid smiled and paced away, alert for further danger. Verelle was gone, but the monsters probably felt no safer in Fairbrook than I had when I'd arrived in Elurien. They were surrounded by their own nightmare creatures here.

Zinian and I helped Auphel sit up. Her bleeding had slowed, but I wasn't going to ask her to move until she felt ready. If the townsfolk were still disturbed by the monsters, that was their problem.

Zinian pulled me a few paces away.

"Do you feel free, now that it's done?" I asked.

He drew in a deep breath of air that had grown thick with pre-rain mist. "I do, but not for that reason. I once thought I was chained to my past as long as Verelle lived. But after you left, I realized that her death wasn't the key I needed." His eyes crinkled in the corners. "It was you. The night we spent together, I lost my chains."

Tears welled up, stinging my eyes, and I nodded. "I know what you mean," I said, my voice hoarse. "Different chains, though."

"I found your letter after you left."

I winced. "You weren't supposed to see that."

"I'm glad I did, though it tore me apart when I realized that I felt the same way about you, and I'd let you go." He grazed my cheek gently with the back side of a curved claw, then leaned in, stopping just before his lips touched mine. "I didn't come here to finish Verelle. I came for you."

I pressed my lips to his, not caring who might be staring.

Somewhere behind us, Auphel let out a weak cheer.

18

If there's one thing to be said for Newfoundlanders (and there are so many things, really), it's that they know how to pick up and carry on after disaster. Verelle had hit the town harder than any winter storm, but the cleanup wasn't so different. The people banded together to rebuild.

Those who still lived, at least.

While the people of Fairbrook had been trapped on the island, a storm had blown in at the other end of the causeway, keeping Verelle's secrets safe. There was much debate over whether to make the story public or cover it up. Would it be good for tourism, or would it frighten people away?

I didn't participate in that discussion, but I did what I could to help while my friends recuperated in the bookstore, well away from the humans. My parents hadn't come to visit us, and things between me and my mother remained uncomfortable at best when we met in town. I doubted I'd ever be forgiven for telling her off. Loretta Walsh knew far better than I how to hold a grudge.

My friends and I spent three more nights in the store, all of us too exhausted to do more than scarf down a meal and collapse into sleep—me from my current hard work, them from their sudden release after years of fighting.

Zinian shared the bed upstairs with me, and sleeping with his arm wrapped around my waist and his breath against my neck was heaven.

"Emergency crews inbound," Gus Hodder commented to me on the third morning. We'd found him hiding under the grocery store's loading dock with a broken leg the evening after Verelle's fall.

"'Bout time," muttered an older man who passed us. He gave me a nod. "Friends still resting?"

"They are."

"Proper thing." He scowled at a Coast Guard helicopter that passed overhead.

The town had kept things quiet until the most important parts of the cleanup were completed. They'd moved bodies to a refrigerated back room of the store. At least the soldiers had disappeared now that Verelle was dead, not leaving so much as a feather behind as proof they'd ever existed.

I kept my eye on a stranger in a black trenchcoat—
a walking cliché of a mysterious government official if
ever there was one. His dark skin appeared flat and
somehow bloodless. He wore a wide-brimmed hat
pulled low over his eyes, but winced and glared
upward as the clouds parted and the sun broke through.
He made me nervous.

I turned toward a rustling noise in the alley behind
me. Zinian stood in the shadows, where they all
preferred to remain, even though many of the
townspeople had tried to offer our legendary
hospitality to them once they'd got over their fears.
Gus gave him a quick nod and hurried away.

"Outsiders are poking around," I said to Zinian as I
walked over. The man in the trenchcoat turned,
squinted into the darkness behind me, and held up one
finger in a clear command.

Stay.

I don't think so. I threaded my fingers between
Zinian's, and we hurried through the alleys toward the
bookstore.

Jaid was waiting on the back step with Tomie, who
had become quite attached to this incredible cat-person
who was able to work the can opener. As it turned out,
his family had been in Florida for the winter, and the
poor fellow had been forgotten in Verelle's chaos. The

spoiled creature would have all the treats he could handle soon enough.

Jaid stood as we approached.

"It's time to go," Zinian said.

"At last," sighed Auphel from inside the store. She squeezed out the door and wobbled a few paces. The hits she'd taken from Verelle had hurt her more than I'd realized, but she would recover. She turned to Zinian with concern written in the creases of her heavy brow. "Did you ask?"

"Not yet."

My heart skipped. I knew what the question was.

Zinian walked toward the park, and I followed. We looked out over the pond. Leaf buds had finally decided to show their faces on some of the trees, giving the park a hazy green cast. Spring was taking its time coming as it always did, with false starts and backward steps, but summer would be glorious when it finally arrived.

"I suppose everyone expects you to stay here," Zinian said, without looking at me.

"They seem to. My uncle is already going on about plans for rebuilding the dairy bar, and I'm sure someone would put me up if things stayed too frosty at home. Things will get better for me here, I think."

People were already treating me differently. Not like the defeated wanderer I'd expected to return as, but a hero.

Zinian nodded sadly. "Not for us, though. We need to leave before more humans come to the island."

"I know." Their work here was done. Asking him to stay for my sake, in a world that would see him as a monster in the most terrifying sense, would be cruel.

He pulled a key from his pocket, big and black and metallic. "If you wanted to come back to visit us, I would leave this with you. I—" He stopped himself, then turned to look at me. His brow furrowed. "The thought of never seeing you again is unbearable to me. I know these people need you, that you belong here, but I can't leave without knowing we'll meet again soon."

"I know," I said again, this time as a whisper that squeaked out around the lump in my throat.

I knew what it would cost him to leave the door open to this world of humans. He would trust me to use the new key well, but as I considered the townspeople, the stranger in the trenchcoat, and the unknown tourists who would soon flood our fair shores, I knew I couldn't expose Elurien to the possibility of them finding it. As much as I wanted to keep the best of both worlds, I couldn't be that selfish.

"The key returns with you," I said. "It's not safe otherwise."

Zinian let out a long breath. "I know that's the right thing," he said. "But it's not what I wanted to hear."

"I'm not finished. I just need a minute to think."

I had come back to Fairbrook out of a sense of duty, giving up my own vague dreams and hazy plans because I couldn't think of anything better to do with my life. And maybe things would be better now if I stayed. But there was another world open to me. Life in Elurien wouldn't be easy for a human, especially one in love with an amalgus. But it would be a life that was worth something. In a world that was busy reinventing itself I could do the same, carving out a position in the city, preserving history and then completing it by recording the other side of the story.

I looked up at Zinian, who watched me with patient expectation. For the first time in my life, I knew what I wanted. No hesitation. No fear.

I stepped closer and placed a hand on his chest. I let my fingers slide over his warm, smooth skin and around his waist, and pulled him to me. "I want you, more than anything," I said. "If you're not too embarrassed to be seen with a human in Elurien, that is. The key returns with you, but so do I."

His smile sent warmth radiating through my chest that was almost painful in its intensity. Maybe we'd face opposition, but we'd change their minds. One at a time if we had to.

"Where will we live?" I asked. "I can't abandon the library, and I've got some ideas for helping out in the city. But you—"

He brushed my hair back and kissed my forehead. "I'm free now. I'll brave the city. I can endure it with you by my side. But perhaps, when you're not too busy, you can see the rest of the world with me."

"Deal." I pulled him into a long, deep kiss and ran my nails over his back from wings to waist. He shivered. "But let's not make it a plan. Let's just see what happens."

We walked through the park together, passing under the crisscrossed shadows of nearly bare branches, and I drank in the beauty of my world for the last time. Leaving it would hurt, but I was ready to let go and leap.

I had other places to be.

Late that night, we followed Jaid to the utility shed in the park. The door had been transformed from a dull metal thing with flaking green paint into an ornate wooden door covered in carvings of birds. I traced my fingers over its surface and tried the purple glass knob.

Locked.

Excitement filled me until I thought it might lift me off the ground. *This is it.*

"Everyone ready?" Zinian asked.

"I was ready before we got here," Jaid said.

Auphel grunted. "I'll still stay at the library?"

Zinian smiled up at her. "I'll see to it that you'll do as you please. You've won your freedom. No more fighting."

"And no Kringus?"

"And no Kringus," he agreed, and reached for my hand. "You're sure about this?"

I grinned back at him. For once, I didn't feel like I needed a lucky charm to get me through. I had everything I needed right there with me.

"Absolutely," I said.

He slipped the key into the lock and turned it. The door swung inward, revealing a dark and foreboding space beyond.

"Ready to fall?" Auphel asked.

I grabbed onto her hand and Zinian's, and he took Jaid's.

"No," I said, and squeezed Zinian's fingers tight. "I'm ready to fly."

Hands in claws, we stepped through the door.

~The End~

Thank you so much for taking the time to read my **Skeleton Key** novella!

All reviews are appreciated.

If you would like to read more from the *Skeleton Key* series, please visit

www.skeletonkeybookseries.com

ABOUT THE AUTHOR

Kate Sparkes lives on the magical island of Newfoundland, where she's always checking wardrobes, locked doors, and interesting caves to see whether they lead to new worlds. She passes the rest of her time hanging out with her family, reading, walking her dogs, and writing fiction that lets her come very close to escaping reality.

She likes sending treats to newsletter subscribers, so be sure to sign up for bonus content, sneak peeks, advance review copies, news about future books, contests, and more! Visit www.katesparkes.com for details.

ACKNOWLEDGEMENTS

Can I just thank *everyone*? No? Okay.

The first big thank yous go to Scarlett Dawn for organizing this amazing book series, and Anthea Sharp for suggesting that I should be a part of it. Without these wonderful writers I never would have met Hazel, Zinian, or Auphel, and I think that would have left my life incomplete.

Next, to the first people who read this story for me and offered reactions: Krista Walsh, Shannon Andrews, and Kathy Dunlavey. Your enthusiasm and suggestions were so helpful. And my beta readers, Stephanie L. Young, Laura Kammerman, Justine Blaber, and Melissa Werbowsky were all so helpful in catching post-edit glitches. Thank you.

To my editor, Sue Archer, thank you for fitting this one into your schedule and doing such a thorough, thoughtful job on edits. I know the word count limit probably made it tough, but you helped so much.

To my cover designer, Jennifer Munswami, thank you for the gorgeous cover art and for your boundless patience.

To my family, thanks for listening to me blabber on about monsters and edits and deadlines, and for letting me get 'er done.

And to my readers... my wonderful, amazing, mind-blowingly enthusiastic readers... thank you for being here, for reading my work and becoming a part of it, for spreading the word about books you love, and for leaving the reviews that are so important to a book's survival in the wilds of book retailers everywhere. You're so incredibly important and appreciated. May every door you open lead to magic and adventure.

-Kate